IT'S
GOOD MORNING
AMERICA

The Last Race

BY
BILLIE BIERER

AmErica House
Baltimore

© 2000 by Billie Bierer.

All rights reserved. No part of this book may be reproduced in any form without written permission from the publishers, except by a reviewer who may quote brief passages in a review to be printed in a newspaper or magazine.

First printing

References

All references to Arabian bloodlines in this novel, *It's Good Morning America,* are fictitious and are not intended to be accurate. The characters and locales although may be correct in location and name are not intended to represent any real occurrences.

ISBN: 1-58851-085-9
PUBLISHED BY AMERICA HOUSE BOOK PUBLISHERS
www.publishamerica.com
Baltimore
Printed in the United States of America

DEDICATION

*This book is dedicated with love to Walter,
my husband and best friend
and our grandchildren, Ryan, Billy, Kyle,
Gabrielle, Hannah and Jacob William*

Acknowledgments

I would like to express my appreciation to the following people who were invaluable to me in writing *Its Good Morning America.*

First, thanks to my husband Walter, who never failed to encourage me.

Second acknowledgment and high fives to my best friend Donna Hartline who is a whirlwind of ideas, who I know had as much fun as I did.

I want to thank my agent Brenda Bailey for walking me through questions and being forever helpful.

And a special acknowledgment to my fantastic filly, GazAnn La Ran who's Dam was twenty-four years young at her foaling. As The Arabian Horse Registry asks, Want to Ride, really ride! Yep!

FOREWORD

*"Nature, when she made the Arab,
made no mistake."*
-Homer Davenport

    The Arabian horse is arguably the most beautiful horse of all; it is unmistakable in character and appearance. It is also the purest and oldest of all breeds, having been carefully bred for thousands of years. While the exact origin of the Arabian is unclear, the evidence from art shows that a race of horses of fixed Arabian type was in existence on the Arabian Peninsula at least 2,500 years before the Christian era. The Bedouin, the people who were most intimately concerned with this 'desert horse', trace their association, from around 3000BC to the Baz, and the stallion Hoshaba. Baz was claimed to have been captured in the Yemen by Bax, the great-great grandson of Noah, tamer of the wild horses. The spread of the all-pervasive Arabian blood throughout the world was made possible by the Muslim conquests, which were initiated by the Prophet Mohammed in the seventh century when the green banners of Islam, and the desert horses, swept through Iberia into Christian Europe.
    During the Crimean War (1851 - 1854), one Arab horse raced 93 miles without harm, but its rider died from exhaustion. This is a story about a stallion called America. A descendent of the foundation mare Baz and the great stallion Hoshaba.

(Excerpts taken from: *The Ultimate Book*; by Elwyn Hartley Edwards 1991)

CHAPTER 1

The beautiful bay mare was wet and lathered her eyes wide with pain as she whirled in the stall. She folded her long legs and went down upon the straw bedding. It was 12:15 a.m. on the fourth of July. Every once in a while the fireworks near town would pop and the sky would light up.

Joe Richards stood deathly still at the stall door watching the mare. He drew each breath quietly. His heart, however, was racing. South Carolina Cicadas chattered wildly outside the barn.

From the hayloft overhead, Joe could hear his father snoring, a sound that could pass for a bear comfortably in hibernation. "Dang," Joe muttered with all the frustration of a thirteen year old boy. "I could use some help here," he said to himself. The mare whirled and folded her legs again. She was down. This time she groaned loudly and lay on her side. With each new contraction she stiffened her legs, pushing. Joe reached behind him quietly and picked up his wooden tray that held his rubber gloves, iodine, scissors, and towel, and slid the stall door latch. He stepped carefully and kneeled behind the mare. The mare raised her head and looked at him, stared into his eyes. Moments passed. It felt to Joe as if her huge brown eyes held his own forever. He rubbed a hand over her haunches. Then with a groan she lay her head down on the sweet straw. "I'm here girl, it's ok," he spoke softly. "Come on now, do your job," he murmured. The mare's legs stiffened and tensed. She flipped her tail over her back. "Good girl, good girl," the boy encouraged the horse. So far, so good, he thought to himself. He slipped on rubber gloves from the tray.

The bear in the hayloft snored loudly again. Joe rolled his eyes and shook his head. His dad just never worried about the mares foaling, but this was the part of the delivery that always scared him. He had assisted mares many times in the last few years. His dad had faith in him, so he shook off the case of nerves that began to surface. Joe knew from the way the mare was acting that she would foal shortly, and he also knew that if anything bad happened he would be able to wake his father.

The mare shifted and rolled up on her back and then back down to her side.

"That's a girl, shift that baby down some," Joe whispered. Suddenly amniotic fluid gushed out. It was then that he could see a hoof in the thin white sack protruding out of the horse. The mare tensed and moved her head up and back, stretching her body its full length. "Come on baby, get out here," Joe murmured. "There they are," he exhaled. Two hooves appeared with a tiny nose resting between as the horse strained once more. Then the mare rested.

Sweat ran down Joe's freckled cheeks and off his forehead into his eyes. He wiped his face on his sleeve. A minute later the mare strained her body once more. "Come on." The shoulders of the foal emerged from the opening and the sack with its great gift flowed from the mare with a glopping rush. The foal's front hoof burst the sack with a small splash. The foal was pushed almost onto Joe's lap. A tiny dark head popped up; two little pointy ears unstuck and big brown eyes fluttered open. Joe sucked in a deep breath and he gingerly touched the new foal.

The foal let out a brave nicker. The mare did not move but she nickered back to the foal just as a few more firecrackers at the stadium popped away. "Happy Fourth of July little guy." Joe said. He began to rub the foal down with a towel. The colt's wet hair was already drying and fluffing. Again the colt nickered. This time the dam raised her lovely head, turned and called loudly to her newborn. "Oh, you did fine girl." He rubbed the mare's hip, holding on to the foal's small body.

"So did you son." His father stood leaning over the side of the stall. "I knew I could count on you to do a good job. I was watching, just wanted you to have this experience. I knew you could handle it. This is going to be your horse, son. What do you want to name him?"

Joe looked at his father. "I think his name should be Fire Cracker, would that be ok?" The mare reached around toward her foal. "Ok mama, just one more minute." Joe poured iodine on the foal's umbilical stub and handed the wooded tray to his father. Joe stood up and the foal tried to follow, but only managed to get close to his mother. Which was just fine with her. Joe backed out of the way. He picked up the afterbirth and put it into a rubber bucket. Together he and his dad examined the afterbirth to make sure it was intact and together, as it should be. This was an important step to ensure the health of the mare. Meantime, the foal with his dam nuzzling needed time to get to know each other. "Fire Cracker." He repeated the chosen name out loud looking at the beautiful bay colt that was already trying to stand. Fire Cracker had the smallest muzzle and the most exquisite neck, with the long lanky legs of a racehorse. Joe knew the horse was going to be special. Clyde put his arm around Joe and both stood and admired the new foal. "Some day," his father said, "you and Fire Cracker will probably do the Tevis Race. I always thought I would do that," Clyde continued, "but it appears not to be in the cards for me. But you, son, you and Fire Cracker would be a winner. I'll help you and you can do it for me." He clapped Joe's shoulder and pulled him toward the house.

"The Tevis Race," Joe thought. "Yeah, Fire Cracker, you and me, just you and me," he smiled.

Glancing above the stall door he read an old Arabic saying inscribed into a rough wooden board: 'Thou shall fly without wings and conquer without swords.' Joe smiled and let his dad lead him away from the best gift ever given him.

1986

Four years later on a day just like any other, Susan Green entered the Richards' ranch house looking for Clyde. She was familiar with the sounds, smells and the comfort of the renovated 18th century two-story dwelling that belonged to her best friend Clyde Richards and his son Joe. The house sat in the middle of one hundred and sixty acres on the outskirts of Camden, South Carolina. Walking through the house, she could smell Clyde's aftershave lingering about, along with the smell of the coffee that he always left half-empty and burning in the pot on the stove. A pair of Joe's dirty socks and old boots were thrown in the corner of the kitchen, waiting to be picked up by a boy too busy with the important things in life to be bothered. She leaned against the counter and looked at a house that was almost too neat for a couple of single men. She loved it here. It was comfortable, just like Clyde. Taking a deep breath she pushed away from the counter, walked across the kitchen, and out the screen door to her parked car. She leaned on the horn impatiently.

Clyde appeared at the barn door and waved to her. She waved back and walked out to the beautifully kept building, admiring the new blue tin roof that Clyde had just put on. She thought it added charm to the horse barn with its great overhanging porch along the entire front of the old barn.

"Hi." Clyde smiled at her. "You're out early this

morning." Taking her arm he led her into the cool shade.

"Well, I could say the same about you," she said.

"Yeah, but it's normal for me to be out early, what's your excuse?" He raised an eyebrow at her. "I have a little project going here," he said. "Figured I better fix this old board on the stall here before one of the horses gets hurt on it. Stand back." Slipping his safety glasses down, he cut a six-by-six board with his electric saw.

"It's as blasted noisy here as it was at my house this morning," Susan yelled. "Which is why I came over here." She plunked down on a nearby bale of straw stacked against the side of the barn wall.

"Oh?" Clyde glanced at her.

"Audrey took a notion to clean the carpets this morning at the break of day. Before coffee, if you can imagine that."

"No, I can't imagine that," Clyde answered without looking up.

"Have you considered that it's cooler early on in the day, Susan? You start early this time of year to get the job done before it gets hot and all. I suppose that's what Audrey had in mind too." He pushed his glasses back down and realigned the boards. "Well Betty home maker you're not. Guess Audrey thought to get her tough chores done before your breakfast an' all." He knew she liked it quiet in the mornings. Her 'thinking time' as she called it.

Susan narrowed her eyes at Clyde. "Nope, no Betty home maker, but I love you anyway," he grinned.

"She interrupted my musings," Susan stated flatly, before he could dismiss her and begin sawing. Clyde pulled his glasses off and looked at her, raising both eyebrows.

"Yes, Clyde, my musings. I find mornings an ideal time for thought." She smiled prettily at him.

"Couldn't be that she roused you from pure laziness, now could it?" Grinning, he hit a couple of nails in the board and fitted it to the stall and finished banging it in. He stepped back and inspected his work. "Yeah, I know what you mean about early morning noise and all," he smiled.

"How about a morning ride? Have you had anything to eat yet? You could rustle us up some bacon and eggs from the kitchen while I saddle us up a couple of outstanding steeds. We could take it with us and have a morning picnic. Of course, you'll have to ride one of my horses."

Susan looked at him in mock horror. There was a running joke between them about which breed of horseflesh was the best. Susan's taste ran to the large Tennessee Walking horse. Clyde preferred Arabians.

"You know, all I have are Arabians. They are the horses that won the crusades. Arabians are a truly nimble animal, not at all like those long-eared mules that can't turn around without tripping on themselves. I think you might change your whole outlook on horses after just this one ride."

"I'll bet," she sneered.

"Ride one and I guarantee you won't be sorry." He walked to a stall and brought out a stout chestnut gelding. "This is Cowboy. He will take you for the ride of your life."

"He isn't crazy, is he?"

"No, actually he is my babysitter. And look, I'm putting you in a real saddle, not some little pancake looking thing." He began saddling the horse. "He takes care of all novices," he said smiling.

"How dare you, Clyde Richards. I do not need a babysitter. I can outride you any day of the week." She laughed and headed for the house to round up the picnic supplies.

Coming back with a knapsack, she handed it to Clyde. "It's funny, as many times as we've ridden together, I've never been on one of your horses. I think I'm going to enjoy this Clyde. I put a thermos of coffee in there, so be careful and don't drop those supplies." Susan stuck her boot into the stirrup and rose into the saddle.

"I want to bring in twenty brood cows from the pasture and put them in with my bull. After breakfast that is." He smiled.

"Well I might have known there was an ulterior motive, but I'm up to a little work. You seem to think I don't do anything of value around my place. How do you think everything gets done over there?" Susan kidded.

"Well, I think all the crew at Magnolia Hill, plus Audrey would be my guess." He laughed. Clyde was saddling a gray. "This is Dandy and he's a little green around cows. He's just a youngster. You'd probably come right off him, and by golly that would mess up your musings for at least a day or two." He laughed as the pretty red-headed woman stuck her tongue out at him. He loved razzing her and getting her in a tizzy. He stepped onto Dandy and rode close to Cowboy, brushing Susan's leg.

"Stay real close, I don't want to have to go hunting a runaway horse with a pretty redhead on him." Nudging his horse he cantered ahead. "You might just change your whole outlook on horses after just this one ride," he yelled back at her. "Is that so?" she yelled, as she nudged her horse to race past him.

Susan had moved to Camden Country twelve years before, after a bitter divorce from an Arkansas politician. "I left Arkansas because I just had to breathe fresh air, and everything there just seems so stagnate, and let's face it an ex-politician's wife is not wanted anywhere. All your old friends suddenly are too busy and the party invitations seem to get lost in the mail. It's better to just start over somewhere else." Her accent drew out each word languidly. She and Joe's Mom Marie had become best friends, even though they were different in every way. They seemed to complement each other. When Marie got sick, Susan would stay days with them, caring for all of them. Without her, Clyde and Joe would not have survived Marie's long illness, and then in the end, her passing. It seemed very natural for the friendship to continue as it had, even blossoming into a little more. She now loved Clyde and she was sure he felt something for her, but she was afraid that anything deeper, like marriage, might kill this wonderful feeling between them. She liked her independence and she couldn't imagine being married to anyone as obsessed with his land and horses as Clyde. Her strong-willed independence kept her free; however, she knew full well that meant she would stay unmarried.

They rode quickly between corrals, then splashed through a small stream at the rear of the fences. Galloping up a wide trail, they came out onto a vast meadow. Steam rose from the grass. The air was heavy and hazy with humidity. Deep blue Asters were blooming across the meadow.

Clyde found a grassy knoll and an unusually large live oak tree and decided this would do for the picnic. He slid from Dandy's back and tossed his reins over a bush. Cowboy had stopped a few feet back and Susan sat looking around. "It is so beautiful here. I just love it." Clyde reached up and lifted her off the horse. Standing close to her stirred a yearning in his heart. She always smelled so fresh, and he knew from dancing with her she fit just right in his arms. He was glad she was here with him. He smiled at her, then turned to gather wood.

Clyde started a small fire and put the bacon in the pan. Susan poured the coffee and handed him a cup. "What wonderful ideas you have Mr. Richards." She smiled, pulling her hair back into a ponytail. The bacon was done and the eggs and bread were cooking in the bacon grease. When finished, he handed her a tin plate and fork. "Just like a fine dining room only better," he said, winking.

After eating and repacking the utensils, Clyde pulled Susan to him and kissed her lightly on her lips. "Can't help myself." He shrugged. "Fresh air, good food, and beautiful scenery always make me romantic."

"Hey mister, who's complaining," Susan answered.

"We had better get back to the chores at hand," he said helping her back on Cowboy. "Are you liking Cowboy yet?"

"I've liked everything about today." She smiled. They rode together side-by-side. "Over there, back among those live Oaks." Clyde pointed. He galloped off to the right in the direction of the bedded cattle. Cowboy followed easily behind. Susan had already begun to appreciate the quiet comfortable gait of the small horse. Cowboy felt plenty strong and was willing to go along nicely at any pace. This was pure heaven.

At the top of the rise, a small breeze lifted her hair and cooled her face and neck. It felt wonderful. The cows had spotted the riders and were slowly getting to their feet, and they began bellowing at the disruption. It was a comforting sound. The herd moved away from the intruders through the speckled shade cast from the huge Oak trees.

"Susan," Clyde yelled. "Ride up to the top of the hill and keep the cows from separating. I'll stay on the bottom side." Susan nodded and moved the gelding 'round to the higher ground. Cowboy seemed to sense what she wanted of him when she shifted her seat in the saddle. Did I just imagine that? She wondered, as she felt the gelding shift direction. They approached a lagging mama cow and calf. The frightened calf darted away from the cow. Susan leaned to her right to place Cowboy on the high side of the calf. Cowboy spun on his rear hocks and headed off the calf. Susan almost came unseated. She was grinning with surprise. Susan had not put pressure on the bit in the horse's mouth and yet he had responded as if he knew her mind. "Well I'll be," she said softly, reaching down to pat the little gelding's neck. This, I could get into, she thought to herself. She wondered if she could learn to really cut cattle like the cowboys? She smiled at the thought.

On their way home, they stopped by the mailbox. Clyde retrieved the morning paper while he was still aboard Dandy. It had been a wonderful picnic and ride.

Clyde put the horses away and they went to the house for a fresh pot of coffee.

"Mmm, smells good," Susan said, as she entered the kitchen. Her skin was glowing from all of the sunshine and the wind from their ride. Her hair gleamed from a brushing and was back to its natural looseness. "I need to call home and make sure Audrey is still there and everything's ok." She reached for the wall phone that hung next to the large table in the breakfast room. Clyde was seated and had flipped open the state's paper. In big print read "TAX REFORM ACT of 1986 SPELL DEATH TO HORSE INDUSTRY?" Clyde quickly scanned the article and looked up at Susan with a horrified expression on his face. Susan quickly hung up the receiver without waiting for an answer and asked, "What is it? What's the matter? You're white as a ghost."

Clyde slapped the paper down on the table. "Well, my throat's just been cut. The big boy's in D.C. have decided to change the tax laws on us."

"What does that mean, Clyde?" Susan asked. His expression was really scaring her.

"Just that if you're an owner of horses, or any livestock, for that matter, you used to be able to be what's called a passive participant," he started to explain.

"Passive? I don't understand." Susan started.

"Wait, let me explain. A person, or a company, could buy an animal, any kind of animal and not really be involved with it. They have someone else take care of it, show it, feed it, and that person or company could write off the expenses against his personal income. Well now that's all changed as of yesterday."

"So how does that affect you?" she said, trying to understand his anger.

"Well, we're active participants, that's true, but our clients are mostly passive participants. If they are passive and decide to dump their animals because they can no longer write off their expenses, their selling will flood the market and eventually kill the horse industry. Man this is going to hurt us." Clyde ran his fingers through his silver hair.

"I still can't see what's got you so upset," Susan frowned.

"Listen Susan, I'm an active participant, but the guys with the big bucks aren't. Lots of rich folks out there enjoy owning an Arabian, showing an Arabian, but don't want to fool with having the work at home. Those were the people paying top dollar for my horses. I make my living off of people like that. Now their expenses can't be written off. It's no longer financially profitable for them to keep this kind of expensive toy around if they can't deduct the expenses from their earned income. The animals that they have been buying are just something to brag about owning while they are sitting around their boardrooms, or the yacht club. I foresee the market flooded and the horse prices hitting rock bottom." Clyde slapped the palm of his big callused hand on the tabletop.

"Everything we have worked for will be gone because some idiot in Washington got a burr under his saddle."

"Yeah," Susan frowned. "Probably, my ex had something to do with this. It sounds like just the sort of thing he could go on TV and tell everyone about: how he is leveling the playing field between the rich and the poor. He's always been full of crap."

"I'm sorry Susan, is this mess going to affect you?"

Clyde said.

"Don't worry about me darlin'. I'll be fine. My income is in a portfolio and I pay a fortune to a very smart manager. I have weathered many a storm. I'm really worried about you and Joe. What will you do now?" Susan sat down beside him and patted his hand.

"Well I won't panic, but I did have an offer from some doctors in California a couple of weeks ago. I'll call them. They wanted my whole herd, if it included Fire Cracker. If I don't take this offer I'm afraid it won't be long until there won't be any offers. I don't think I could hold on to our land if that happens." Clyde was speaking softly, almost a whisper.

"No!" Susan yelled. "Don't do anything that drastic. Don't sell your horses. You certainly can't sell Joe's horse. He would never forgive you. It's too harsh a step, Clyde. Just wait a while and see what happens with the market." She was pleading.

"If I don't sell Fire Cracker then they don't want the rest of the herd. I'm back where I started. Fire Cracker is the main draw." Clyde got up from the table and stood at the window. He could see Fire Cracker walking around in the pasture directly in front of the house. "Susan, they don't want the mares without him. He's more important than the mares, and the mares were picked just for their complimenting bloodlines. I'll have to make Joe understand, that's all. He'll just have to understand what the priority is."

"Joe might be mature for his age, but he will not understand. Trust me on this Clyde. He won't understand. You have to find another way." The fine lines that etched around her large brown eyes deepened. Two hours ago, her eyes had crinkled with laughter; now she looked sad. Susan didn't have to worry about money, Clyde realized. She had been born to money, survived a divorce, and still came out ahead. She wouldn't understand the gut-wrenching pain Clyde felt at the thought of losing the farm.

"Joe knows we are in the horse business, and if I don't jump on this sale now, we could end up real losers. I cannot jeopardize this farm for any reason. Sure, selling his horse will hurt, but Joe knows that this farm and this land come first. We'll go back to farming, grow hay and wheat straw. It's what we used to do and we can do it again by damn," Clyde said.

"Clyde, you are wrong. I can see how important all this is to you." She threw her arms out. "But Clyde, Joe is a hell of a lot more important than all of this. Don't do anything that will come between you two. Trust me, I've lost a lot in my life; there is nothing, not land not money, nothing is more important than what you have with Joe." Susan stood up and crossed to him, kissing him lightly. "Think about it, please, before you make a final decision."

Turning, she walked briskly across the room and pushed the screen door open.

"My family kept this farm going for over one-hundred years, through the Depression. I can't be the one to lose it. Joe will have to understand." Clyde's eyes were narrow and dark.

Susan came back and looked at him. "Let me loan you some money. I have plenty of money. The market will probably come back fast, and even if it doesn't, hell, it's only money," Susan pleaded.

"I can't take your money. It would be like stealing from you. I can't do that." Clyde was shaking his head.

"Clyde Richards," she threw her hands up, "you are so damned hard-headed. If that boy needs a shoulder, you send him over to me. I'll try to help as much as I can, but I think you're taking it too lightly about the pain that Joe is going to feel." Clyde pushed away from the counter and put his arms around her, hugging her up close to him. Walking her to the door, "Better go get Audrey to make those good brownies. I am sure Joe will be banging on your door soon. If not him, then me; either way, you're going to be having company." He squeezed her. "Thanks for being there for us." Susan nodded and went out the back door, stopping on the flagstone walkway to look at the old-fashioned pink roses growing along the pathway. She looked to the rolling fields of Richards' Arabians on her right. Live oaks mixed with red Oaks dotted the pastures.

Mares and foals were grazing in the hazy morning light. Land was a thing to hold on to in the south. But a son like Joe Richards was worth losing it all for. She understood that Clyde felt his place was a refuge, a safe haven for his family. What he didn't realize was that without that boy, the land and the farm didn't matter.

Joe was in the barn cleaning the stalls when he heard the screen door slam. He walked to the barn door, and seeing Susan, he hollered and waved to her. Waving back, Susan thought, yes everything in this world changes and there are times when we have to do things that we would rather not do, but it's a sorry day when that boy is told he's going to lose his horse. She didn't believe that Joe would ever forget this day, not in his entire life. "Lordy, Lordy," she said out loud and continued to her Suburban parked in the driveway.

"No, no way, I won't let you sell him." Joe yelled at his Dad. "He's my horse, you gave him to me. On the day he was born you said he was mine. You can't sell what's not yours." Joe started for the door and Clyde caught him by the arm.

"Don't talk to me like that," Clyde said. "This is not something that I want to do. Do you think I like turning our lives upside down? Do you think I like going back on my word? You sit down here at the table and you tell me how else I can save this place if you're so smart." Clyde was feeling sick. The last thing he wanted was Joe not understanding the severity of the problem.

Joe sat down heavily on the chair and laid his head on the table. "But why him?" he pleaded. "Sell all the rest, I'll work hard, I won't go to college, I'll get a second job in town, we'll make it. Just let me keep Fire Cracker."

"He's the only reason they are willing to buy the entire herd. Without him, the deal won't go through. I turned down the offer when it first came, but now I have no choice. I've always told you that our horses were our business. It's never been an easy business. Our horses were an investment and our livelihood. As long as we could earn money at it I figured we could keep doing what we loved to do. I told you over and over not to forget that, no matter how much you love them, or how much you love Fire Cracker. We had to be able to earn a living raising the horses." Clyde had spoken quietly hoping to smooth the hurt he knew Joe was feeling.

"Fire Cracker is the foundation of our bloodline. You told me that dad. He's the best of the best. He is the most important horse we have ever had here. If we sell him, we won't have anything left." Joe was crying now, his face splotchy and swollen.

"You're not hearing me Joe. If I don't sell the horses, including Fire Cracker, we could lose the farm. It will be all I can do to just keep us afloat. I know this is hard for you to understand, but we need income. I will not lose this land just to be able to raise horses people don't want. Clyde's voice was raspy; his words sounded hollow even to him.

"These are the best damned endurance horses ever and Fire Cracker is the best of all of them and he hasn't even gotten his chance to prove it." Joe shouted through his tears.

Clyde let the cussing slide. He knew the boy was losing more than just a horse. Fire Cracker was not just any horse to his boy. "What about all our plans?" Joe sobbed. "What about the Tevis race?"

"We'll make new plans. The Tevis will be there. Just remember that if we keep the land, we will still have a way to dream. This country is full of folks a whole lot worse off than we are." Clyde got to his feet ending the discussion. He walked toward the kitchen, his throat felt raw and dry. He needed a drink of water. Joe knew his dad was through talking, but he couldn't stop.

"He fell into my arms when he was born," he screamed at his father.

"I know," Clyde answered, then to himself, "I know."

His son was already gone. Joe stomped through the kitchen and out the back door, slamming it hard. Clyde hated losing control of their lives, of his son's future. He hated that he couldn't make the loss easier for Joe. He hated that he had not seen this coming. He knew that feeling of being in control of one's destiny was just that, a feeling and shaky at best...being totally powerless was what he hated most. He wondered if he hadn't just lost a lot more than his horse farm. Suddenly he just felt old.

That night in his room with the window open, Joe looked at the stars and thought of the four years that he'd had with Fire Cracker. The horse had been the most wonderful friend he could have had. Fire Cracker was born a nobleman among horses. Of course, Joe conceded he could have been a little barn blind about Cracker. He remembered the halter shows that he had entered with him and Cracker had done ok. He had usually placed in the top five entries. But judges wanted other qualities in a halter stallion; this always puzzled Joe because every time he studied the old pictures of the ancient Arabians from Egypt, in his books all he saw was Cracker looking back at him. Times were changing the appearance of the Arabian horse in America; even a kid could see that. Personal preferences and big money seemed to be determining the characteristics that folks were breeding for. Joe didn't think much of personal opinions. He figured after five thousand years of breeding the most beautiful Arabians man ever saw, the horse's original beauty didn't need changing. To him, the Arabian horse was proof that there was perfection in the world. Fire Cracker had been Joe's proof. His dream of racing him in the tradition of the

Bedouin tribesmen in the Tevis was gone. Fire Cracker had run for the sheer joy of the race. Joe had always known in his heart that no other horse could beat him. He would have been the best of the best. Joe remembered racing him through the pastures, riding him low and fast, the stallions' mane whipping his face as he clung to him, tears flowing from his eyes blurring his vision. He could still feel the great leaps and the surge of power under him as they flew over the ground. He would never forget that feeling of power. How could he get over this horse he loved so much? Because of a law, he could no longer have what he loved. How could something as stupid sounding as that happen? He thought of his mother as he sat looking into the night sky from the window of his room. He often felt her presence but didn't know if he felt it in his heart, in his mind, or if she was really there somewhere watching him. Please just help me understand this, he prayed. He knew he was going have to say goodbye to his friend.

CHAPTER 2

Joe turned eighteen the week that Fire Cracker walked up the ramp of the twelve-horse-van that came to transport him to his new home in California. Joe's truck was packed and waiting in the driveway. His gear was tied down with a bright orange tarp. He was heading for Clemson University in the upstate of South Carolina.

He used the University for a diversion for the emptiness in his heart. Joe dug into the academic work at the university taking course work in summers, too. He realized all the while he was avoiding going home. He missed his father, his house, his very own room upstairs. Mostly he missed his horse. He even admitted to missing the hick town where he grew up and often made fun of. Joe buried himself in studies, working his brain much as he had worked his body on the farm. In the end, it paid off. He graduated in three and a half years with a degree in Mechanical Engineering. Had he not lost himself in his work at school. He didn't know what would have become of him. He didn't enjoy crowds, and he had been too busy for a social life.

Joe came home twice during those three and a half years. He hadn't gone to the barn one time during those visits. It was now the fall of 1988 and he was driving his F150 down I-85 heading home. He sighed heavily. He was edgy and unsure of this homecoming. Now that he was through with school, he'd be home until he found a job. Home was where the memories of Fire Cracker lingered. He hoped to get a quick response from the interview he'd had with MCI the previous week. Maybe he'd be home only a short while.

Bright yellow, red, and orange colors flashed past his window. He rolled down the truck window. The air was clean and fresh. Less humidity and clear air meant the coming of fall in the upstate. It was time to get over his losses and start his own life. He felt ready to be grateful for what he had and stop the nonsense about what he didn't have. He'd just had his first job interview for heaven sake. He felt pretty decent about it too. Maybe he'd hear from them soon. Ok—Ok he said out loud. He turned east on I-26 and set his cruise at seventy. He was on his way home.

"Man it's hot, Dad. Funny how I forgot summer isn't over down here in September at home."

"Here, wet down that shirt, son." Clyde smiled. Joe stripped his sweaty tee shirt off. Clyde tipped the big silver ten-gallon water cooler that was sitting on the tailgate of his old blue truck over on its side and poured. When the shirt was wet through, Joe struck his head under the cold water, popped his head up, and shook it like a half drowned pup. Clyde laughed out loud. His son had changed but not in every way.

"Nope, the hot weather in September ain't changed a bit, though you have son. Look at you all muscled out with a college degree, too. You're not my kid any more, you're a man." He looked at Joe earnestly. "It's real good to have you home, son. I'm right proud of you, and your mother would have been, too." Clyde's blue eyes sparkled in the bright fall sunlight.

"It's good to be here dad," Joe said. He swiped his brow with the wet shirt and put it on.

"Whelp," Clyde said a little to heartily, "Might just as well get the rest of these bales loaded and to the barn. I'll turn the hay on the back twenty in the morning to dry. Probably be able to bale it in the afternoon, if this weather holds. It's always the hottest day when your doin' hay," he chuckled at his own joke. "This is real good hay son. We should get a good price for it this season."

"You know it," Joe agreed. Clyde drove the truck forward while Joe loaded and stacked the bales. Joe's muscles felt tired, but it was good to be doing this labor, real good. The leaves were changing and a frost would soon be coming. Joe felt more alive and in touch than he'd felt in a long, long time. It was good to be home.

He'd been home three weeks when it came. He saw the large white envelope lying on the kitchen table unopened. Then he saw his name. Mr. Joseph Richards it said. It was from MCI, Greenville, S. C. Joe grabbed a jug of Gatorade from the fridge and sat at the table. He moved the envelope directly in front of him and drank from the green bottle. He stared at the envelope, sat down his drink, and tore it open.

Dear Mr. Richards:
I have enclosed a contract of employment for your review. If you are in agreement with the terms of employment, please sign and date where indicated. Return the original to this office by October the twenty-fifth, 1989.

I look forward to hearing from you. Your education would be a tremendous asset to our company. We would be proud to welcome you to the MCI family of corporate employees.
Sincerely,
Rodger Davis, Human Resource Manager

    The interview had seemed slick at the time. He had wondered if he'd actually been hired before he had shown up for the meeting. When they met him they had simply approved the body that came with the degree. It looked like he had a job. Now he had the dilemma of telling his father. Of course he had to. He knew his father expected it sooner or later.

    That evening when Clyde came in for supper, Joe said, "I'm going to Greenville Saturday morning dad. I have to look for a place to live. Looks like I've been gainfully employed."

    "Whoa." Clyde looked at Joe. "When did all this happen?"

    "Well I interviewed with MCI before I came home. I didn't mention it because, well, you never know what's going to happen."

    "You'll be moving then?"

    "Guess so."

    "Well," Clyde said, "how much?"

    "How much?"

    "Yes son. How much are they going to pay you?"

    "Oh." Joe got his contract from the table. "$42,500 to start."

    "A year?"

"Yes dad."

Clyde whistled. "That's real good. A heck of a lot better than selling hay, I reckon."

"Yeah, maybe so," Joe said. Why did he not feel joy in his heart over this new and fantastic job? he wondered.

CHAPTER 3

The telephone startled Clyde out of a deep sleep.

"Lo," he mumbled.

"Is this Mr. Richards? Clyde Richards?" a deep unfamiliar male voice asked.

"Speaking," Clyde said. He pulled the brass chain on the light on the nightstand next to his bed. "Who's this?" Clyde asked somewhat indignantly.

"Jack McDonald here, attorney for Suwalli Enterprises here in Oakland, California. Mr. Richards, I believe you sold an Arabian stallion, Fire Cracker, registration #463086 to these gentlemen: Mr. Lloyd Sims, Davis Lowe, Bennett Douglas and Dr. Keith Thomas. I have a copy of your contract here before me."

"Ah, what was your name? Donald?"

"McDonald, Mr. Richards."

"Yeah, McDonald. Look, do you know what time it is in South Carolina, McDonald?"

"Yes, and I do apologize for the inconvenience, Mr. Richards, may I call you Clyde?"

"No." Clyde answered.

"Well, Mr. Richards, I'm afraid I have some bad news. The syndication has been liquidated as of today at 4p.m. California time. The legal documents were tidied up and the syndication has gone on record filing Chapter 13 bankruptcy."

35

"Wait a minute, McDonald. I don't think it's all that tidy. The syndication still owes Richards' Arabians one payment of $200,000." Clyde was now awake. He slid his legs over the edge of the four poster bed and put his feet into the sheep skin moccasins that were always neatly placed there. "$200,000 is not a tidy matter to sweep away with a bunch of papers." He was on the way into the kitchen, heading for the coffee pot.

"Yes, well, the syndication is prepared to auction Fire Cracker off to the highest bidder at the Oakland Livestock Symposium on April the 15th at 12 noon, California time. All proceeds will be forwarded to Richards' Arabians via electronic wire, Mr. Richards. Under the current California state statutes, that is the best that we can do. However, we must be in receipt of the animals signed original registration in order to fulfill this court order." There was silence on the line. "Mr. Richards?" Then ...

"Over my dead body," Clyde said. "I want him back."

"We thought about that Mr. Richards. The agreement is that in the event that you want to reclaim said horse, the syndication requires that you sign a certified agreement that you have the animal gelded upon arrival at your farm, say, within thirty days. We feel that is reasonable time."

"I see you bastards have thought of everything."

"If you agree to this. You may contact me after signing the agreement, which I will send overnight mail to you. I must emphasize that you will have to overnight your signed copy back to me to cancel the upcoming auction."

"You guys just sit around on your fat asses all day and night figuring this stuff out, don't you?" Clyde was furious. He'd never been so angry in his life.

"Actually, Mr. Richards, it was a difficult emotional decision."

"Yes, I can tell," Clyde said, but his mind was already planning. "Jack, just where are they keeping my horse these days?"

"He's being well taken care of, I assure you. They have him at their stable in Oakland, in fact. He will not be moved until the day of the auction, in the event that we hear from you. It is in their best interest to treat this horse very well."

"Oh? Well I'll get back to you Jack."

"I stress, Mr. Richards, a speedy reply is of the essence. My number here is area code 912-744-5500. We'll be awaiting your reply." Clyde wrote down the attorney's number for all the right reasons.

"Sure," Clyde answered.

The coffee was perking. Clyde filled his mug. No way was this going to happen. No way. He walked into the room where he had kept Fire Cracker's papers all these years tucked neatly in his file folder. Clyde opened it. Cracker's registration papers lay there, the gold registration seal gleaming in the reflection from the overhead light.

"You're coming home Cracker, by damn, or I'll die trying to get you here," he swore.

Clyde pulled on his jeans and got a clean flannel shirt out of the closet. He called Susan.

"Hi honey. I'm sorry to get you up. I need a favor."

"Gosh, Clyde are you alright?" Susan asked sleepily.

"I've got to go out to California. I'm going to try to pick up Fire Cracker. The doctors are out of business. I just got a call from their attorney. They want to auction him off on the 15th of this month."

"Clyde that's just three days from now."

"Yeah. Unless I agree to have him gelded, which is not going to happen, they will resell him to the highest bidder. They owe me $200,000 on the last payment and I'm going to get my horse. I'm leaving as soon as I can load up."

"Tonight?"

"Yes."

"I'll get ready."

"No I need to do this alone. I never should have sold him. It was a terrible regret from the start and maybe I can make things right again. I'll take my phone and call you. Do me a favor, though, and call Joe, will you. Don't tell him I've gone after Fire Cracker. Just tell him I had business and I'll be home next week some time. Tell him you'll call him later after I know more. I just need to buy some time before I tell him what's going on, hon."

"Ok sure. You be careful Clyde. The highway is dangerous, especially out there."

"Not near as dangerous as these over-zealous lawyers running this country," he said. "I'll keep you posted. I'll need a lot of help from the guy above most likely."

Clyde backed the truck up to the two-horse trailer. He was sure glad he'd kept new tires on the truck and trailer. He took out the stall divider to make the area roomier for Cracker, threw in two bales of good, clean hay and a rubber bucket. He put his suitcase up front on the floorboard of the truck along with a gallon jug of water. He checked his wallet. He had five hundred cash and a credit card with a one hundred thousand dollar limit. He figured that would do. It was 3 a.m. Clyde's 60th birthday was two weeks away. If he could pull this off, it would be a heck of a birthday present.

Thirty hours later, one April 15th at 1 a.m., the Suwalli ranch house came into view. It had not been all that difficult to find. It was off of highway 15 on Del Rio Drive, then north about two miles. The guard station and the giant gold statue gleaming under a night light beside the gaudy spouting waterfall gave it away. There was trash and litter blown around the guard station. Clyde didn't think security was real heavy. He cruised past the guard station. The asphalt drive was lined with more bronze statues of Turks and Barbs on Arabians doing battle. He could almost hear the thundering hooves.

"Must be more statues here than Rome itself," Clyde mumbled.

He drove on past a long dark ranch house. The drive was full of fallen palm fronds blown from the trees and left to rot. Then he spotted the barn. The outline of it was long and low, with hedgerows planted along the front, except where the double doors entered the barn walk. He held his breath. If anyone were about, they would probably be back here. He pulled the truck and trailer behind the hedge and cut the engine. He rolled down his window and sat listening. Nothing. Stepping from the truck he whispered,

"Where are you boy?"

There was one light bulb glowing down near the center part of the barn.

"If you were mine," Clyde said, "I'd put you in the center, not on the outside." A breeze whispered through old cottonwood and eucalyptus trees behind the barn. The scent of mint was in the air. Clyde was thinking that the place was probably pretty nice, maybe two hundred years ago. He shivered, and the hair on the back of his neck prickled. He was tense and his stomach hurt from too much coffee and too little food. He moved down the row toward the yellow glow. "Cracker," he whispered. Magically, a soft nicker answered him.

Fire Cracker was standing backed into the far corner of the stall, and even in the low light Clyde could see the evil that they had done. He felt sick.

"Oh Cracker what have they done?" he spoke softly. The big bay lifted his head. His ears came forward. The horse's body was emaciated, even his lovely head was sunken and huge hollow indentations were above both of the horse's great luminous eyes. Clyde moved swiftly, slipped the halter over the horse's head without a thought or hesitation, and led him toward the waiting trailer. He had only glanced at the stallion, but he knew no one would have gotten a plug nickel for this horse at an auction.

"Bastards," he said. He only prayed that Cracker would survive the trip home. Clyde loaded the horse and returned the way he had driven in.

Clyde had driven an hour down the road. Coming into Redlands, Clyde saw a sign advertising a veterinarian with a sign that included the picture of a horse. He pulled in. Doc, as he preferred to be called, stood scratching his prematurely bald head. They were both looking at Fire Cracker.

"He's about one hundred fifty pounds underweight. That isn't the worse news, however. He has blood in his urine. That worries me a lot more. I can't tell you more without further testing, which would take days. Mr. Richards, to be honest, I'm not sure this horse has days. I'm sorry."

Clyde didn't have days either. He placed a call to Dr. Cindi Arders back home and explained his situation to her. He also told her he was about twenty-seven hours from her door, but to please keep it open for him and that he would call her as soon as he got close.

Doc sent Clyde off with tranquilizers, electrolyte paste and salt tablets.

"You have to keep him drinking. It's the most important thing," he told Clyde. "Please sir, I'd like to know if he makes it." The young doctor pushed away Clyde's hand that held money. "God's speed." He smiled. "For the record, I will document your visit and my findings this morning. Also, I will document where the horse was kept and the names of the people whose care he was in. I wish I could do more for him, Clyde, but maybe you can use the information I record some time in the future." He handed Clyde a business card.

"How's the x-ray look, Dena?" Dr. Cindi Arders was calm, and during the fifteen years that Dena Louis had been Dr. Arders veterinary assistant, calm and cool always meant the worst. Dena clipped the black shiny film up to the film display. Dr. Cindi stopped in front of the screen and they both stared quietly at the film.

"There's the problem," Dena said and pointed with the tip of her closed ink pen.

"This isn't good," Dr. Cindi sighed. She was slim and narrow-hipped, built much like a young boy instead of the forty-year-old woman that she actually was. She was smart and quick. Her veterinary practice was the most renowned equine reproduction practice in the Eastern U.S. Dr. Cindi was simply the best at what she did.

"We're going to lose this guy. He's had way too hard a life for such a fine animal. Did you notice the rope scar on his neck and the cut and gash scars on his legs?"

"Yes doctor," Dena replied.

"My gosh." Dr. Cindi swiped her arm over her forehead. "How in the world will I tell Clyde that his efforts to reclaim his horse were in vain?" Joe Richards was one of her very favorite horse people. Had he had more schooling, she had no doubt he would have been an Olympic class rider. She had watched Joe grow up on the Richards' endurance bred Arabians. She knew how important Fire Cracker was to them. When Clyde sold Fire Cracker to the syndication she had heard that father and son had grown apart. For heaven's sake, Cindi had given the colt his first vet exam and inoculations. Dr. Cindi looked sharply down the isle of her ten-stall barn.

"Dena," she nearly shouted, "bring Bint." Dena jumped from Cindi's tone of voice, strode over, grabbed a halter and lead from the tack hanger, and went to the third stall on the right side of the barn. A soft nicker greeted her. Cindi met Dena in the aisle way leading a small bay Arabian mare. Dena's expression was one of confusion.

"I know, I know, don't say it. I've already changed my mind. Maybe it won't even work, but I've got to at least try."

"I didn't utter a sound, Doc." Dena made a face and rolled her big brown eyes.

"You didn't have to."

Bint Nefsoud was much past her prime of life and Cindi wanted to try to get her in foal to preserve her wonderful Bedouin bloodlines. She had planned to breed her to a stallion from Minnesota; in fact she had the frozen semen in the refrigerator. She had paid dearly for the stud fee plus the transport. Suddenly it seemed a very good idea to try to get her in foal to Fire Cracker. This idea would be a gamble and it would be critical timing. Number one, she didn't know if Fire Cracker was up to mounting the dummy mare. She was about to find out. The horse's time on earth was now measured in hours.

"Ok, let's walk down here and see what this guy thinks of our girl," Cindi said.

"Ok," Dena said and they led her to Fire Cracker's stall door.

"Maybe we can save something of Fire Cracker," she smiled hopefully.

Bint Nefsoud called to Fire Cracker through the stall window. It was a huge call, not a small whinny. The whole barn was suddenly alive with horse talk. The bay stallion's head came up, small pointed ears pricked forward, and he trotted to the stall door. Two sets of large brown eyes gazed longingly at the other. Fire Cracker arched his long graceful neck and talked to the mare. His hoof hit the bottom of the stall door in anticipation. Dr. Cindi and Dena smiled at each other.

"What about all the money you spent on that stud fee?" Dena stroked the mare's shoulder.

"It's frozen and on hold, it will work out. I know this will work out," she grinned. "Let's get old ugly set up,"

Cindi said. "We got business to tend to." Dr Cindi grabbed the mineral oil and the disposable AV (Artificial Vagina) sleeves. She pulled her tin plastic gloves from the shelf. There would be no delay with the procedure that she was preparing to do. No lost time. This was Fire Cracker's time, and hopefully with the help of the guy upstairs and a lot of luck this would work.

Bint Nefsoud waited patiently in front of the dummy mare. Fire Cracker was alert now, considering his complications, as Dena led him forward toward the dummy and collection setup.

"Come on boy," Dena murmured to the horse. Bint greeted them with excitement, her tail up over her back. She didn't look eighteen years old. Ten minutes later, Dr. Cindi was looking into the microscope at her slide sample.

"Well," she grinned, "we certainly have got some live critters here." She spun around on the stool, jumped off, and gave Dena a high-five.

"Let's fix up the old girl," she laughed.

At eleven p.m. that night, Cindi sat cross-legged beside Fire Cracker on the floor of his stall. Cracker had his head on her lap. She was stroking his lovely neck. It was as if he knew he had done all he could and had simply given up. Cindi put Fire Cracker to sleep to ease his way.

When it was over, and he drew his last breath, Cindi went out of the barn and sat on her wood bench looking at the stars and listening to the cicadas. She wondered, as she often did at times like this, if horses have souls like people, and if they did, would the good ones be honored in heaven? She hoped so.

"Clyde," Cindi said into the receiver, "Cracker is gone. I had to euthanise him early this morning. I'm so sorry Clyde, really I am."

"Damn," was all Clyde could say.

"Listen, Clyde, we bred my mare Bint Nefsoud last night to Fire Cracker. I was able to retrieve a healthy vial AI and we got her covered. She happened to be conveniently in season."

"You did?" Clyde couldn't believe what he was hearing.

"Yes. Now I know that there could be legal repercussions, for both of us possibly, but it just seemed the right thing to do. Anyway I'll take full responsibility, Clyde, I just wanted you to know that."

"But," he started.

"Wait, before you say anything else. We won't know if she took for fourteen days, well, thirteen now. That's the earliest I can tell with my ultra sound machine."

"I love you doc," Clyde said.

"Clyde, don't tell Joe yet. It's way too early, and AI is sometimes iffy. Besides, we are dealing with an aged mare here. Bint is eighteen now. But she's the best darn Arab I've ever had and I was going to breed her myself. By golly, I hope this works. I have a very good feeling about it."

"Doc, Joe doesn't even know I went to California to get Fire Cracker. Maybe now it would be better if he didn't know, till later."

"That's probably best, you're right. It'll be our secret for a while. Let's see if this works." Cindi smiled into the receiver. She did have a good feeling about this.

CHAPTER 4

"For sale by owner, 10 acres, backs up to Sumter National Forest. $27,500." The ad didn't mention how you had to get into the property that was listed with Greenville Real Estate Sales. Red Barron; Joe didn't know if the name was an indication of something unforeseeable, past or present, that would meet him at the intersection of highway 11 and 130 outside of Greenville. It was a Sunday afternoon, and by Sunday evening he had a signed copy of the contract in front of him.

The property, as it turned out, was thirty-seven miles from the MCI Corporate offices, but he didn't care. It was the most beautiful ten acres that he had ever seen and it was his. The parcel, which was rectangular-shaped, backed up on the northeastern edge of Sumter National Forest in the Cherokee foothills. He didn't know how he had lucked out, but he figured the mile of four-wheel drive road had something to do with it.

"Don't ya think this is a scenic old road?" Red Barron laughed as they bounced along in 4-wheel drive granny gear.

"Yes sir." Joe laughed hitting his head on the roof liner of his truck.

The rutted road opened up into the center of a pristine grassy meadow that had a stream flowing through the center of it. Joe couldn't drag his eyes away from the pretty view. He stopped the truck and sat looking at the land, while the realtor sitting beside him on the truck seat was most likely already counting up his commission.

The whole of the property encircled the meadow. The forest surrounding the meadow was a mixture of pine and hardwoods, and along the stream there were mountain laurels. The back of the property that ran along the Forestry land was abundant with the laurels. The top side of the meadow was the perfect spot for a cabin, and the meadow just invited a small barn with a couple of paddocks. With the national forest behind, the property was a perfect setup for having a couple of horses. Joe didn't know much about the general area, but he fully intended to explore it as soon as he started construction of the cabin he envisioned sitting in the meadow.

The very next weekend after the deal closed, Clyde drove up and Joe met him out on the highway. They drove into the ten acres in Joe's truck. Joe stopped the truck at the edge of the meadow and Clyde got out and stood looking at the property.

"Well, don't suppose there will be many women showing up around here." He took off his cap and rubbed his head, then chewed some on his worn toothpick. After a hesitation he added, "But, I reckon if you brought one in here, they'd have a time escapen'." Clyde smiled like maybe this was a good idea after all.

"Well that sums it up then, right dad?" Joe said a little short.

"Naw it's a right pretty spot son. But I was always hoping you'd stay in Camden I guess."

"For now I need to be here to make some money dad."

"Yeah, I know that," Clyde said. "You stay out of debt, it won't take much to do what you want to do in your life."

"Well you taught me that alright," Joe said with a sigh. Stay out of debt at all costs, he was thinking. Don't want any debt-only income. Where had he heard those words before? Joe thought that sometimes you had to step out and take a few chances, though, or you'd miss out on life. He thought these things, but he didn't say them, not now. He was starting new; he didn't want any bad feelings. He was just going to step out and take one of those chances.

Three tiers up, on wooden scaffolding, Joe was nailing tongue and grove oak to the eighteen-foot ceiling of his log cabin. The room was twenty-by-twenty. It was no small task, and sweat ran down the sides of his unshaven face. The white tee shirt he had on was wet and the logo JUST DO IT was the only part that wasn't stuck to him.

The nail gun popped and he stepped over a foot and pulled the trigger again.

The telephone on the desk in the far corner of the room began to ring. He stepped over a foot and pulled the trigger on the nail gun. Another pop filled the room. He turned and stared at the telephone.

"Ok, ok." By the fifth ring he was swinging to the floor. Three huge steps and he grabbed the receiver.

"Lo?"

"Hey Joe, Cindy here."

"Oh hey Doc, how's it going?"

"Great, great. Listen if you could come down to Camden tonight, I'm having a family get together and I wanted to include your family. We're grilling burgers and stuff and I'd like to share some good news with you."

"Say, that's really nice." Joe frowned. He was thinking that this was odd, but he didn't say it. Doc Cindi had been the farm vet for his father for a long time and they considered her a good friend, but they had never been socially involved with her family.

"Well I can sure use good news Doc. What time do you want me there?"

"How is seven o'clock?"

"Ok, that will be just fine."

"Great, we know how hard you have been working. I'll be done with my appointments and we can enjoy ourselves."

"Can I bring something?" He hadn't totally forgotten his manners.

"Well, I think a good bottle of wine would be excellent. This is a very special occasion." She was smiling into the receiver on the other end.

"Well, ok, then I'll do it. I'm looking forward to it."

"By the way your father and Susan will be here about seven also."

"Good," he said, wondering what in the world was going on.

"See you tonight then," she said, and Joe hung the phone up looking at it puzzled.

Oh well, he thought, good news. He looked at the half-done ceiling above and burst into his rendition of the old song, "Feelings."

"Ceilings whoa, whoa, whoa ceilings," he wailed. Then he climbed the scaffolding to continue nailing. He knew he'd have to be on his way at four that afternoon. It was a three-hour drive to Doc's place from Greenville.

At seven he was driving his ford ¾ ton truck down Dr. Arders lane. He could see his dad's old Ford sitting behind the house, along with several other cars. Smoke was coming from the barbecue nestled between a triangle of one-hundred-year-old oaks that shaded the yard and the outside paddocks that joined the barn. It was a lovely, peaceful setting. A swing set with two swings hung on heavy six by six's stood under one tree.

There was a large graceful swimming pool lined with boulders, and a waterfall on one end splashing into the blue water of the pool.

As Joe was getting out of his truck, Cindi greeted him. "This is sure a beautiful spot Doc. I didn't realize how pretty it was out here."

"Thanks Joe." Cindi accepted his bottle of wine and gave him a friendly hug. Two other people stepped up behind her. "You know Joel, my husband, and this is my new assistant, Denneyse Danner." Joe smiled at the tall young woman, and as she stepped forward he shook her out-stretched hand. The young woman had on a Clemson baseball cap pulled low on her forehead. A very long sandy brown ponytail, parts of which were floating in the breeze, hung out of the back of her cap. She had on a navy tee shirt with a Nike emblem and faded jeans with tennis shoes. Her eyes were green as a cat's. She had no makeup on, that he noticed.

"Hi," he said. "Another Clemson fan I see," he smiled.

"Good to meet you." She grinned, showing perfect white teeth and a pretty smile. She had a sprinkling of freckles across her nose. She wasn't beautiful, but the barbecue had definitely become more interesting.

"Cindi speaks of you often, Joe," Denneyse said. Cindi interrupted.

"You remember Josh and Lynn over there by the picnic table—our kids and your dad's over there shooting the breeze about the Braves game last night," she laughed.

"We'll probably have a small wager going before it's over." Joe waved to the seniors lounging in the chaise lounges under the oaks. "The food will be ready in thirty minutes, Joe, but first I want you to come with me." Cindi touched his elbow steering him in the direction of her barn.

Doctor Cindi Arters told Joe the whole story on the way to the barn. Joe stopped walking and looked at her when she got to the part when they lost Fire Cracker. There was a troubling sadness in his eyes.

"When Cracker was sold, I would console myself with the thought that he was leading a life of ease with lots of mares to breed and lots of good food. This puts an end to all of my fantasies."

"Sometimes we can only do the best we know how, Joe. Things happen that we can never understand or explain. You can have one more now though," she said.

"What do you mean?"

"One more chance to dream, Joe." They had arrived in front of a paddock and Cindi whistled. Magically from within the barn came a rustling and a wondrous brown mare burst from the doorway into the fenced paddock area. Her tail was flagging high as she trotted the length of the fence and stopped dead in front of them. The creature standing in front of him demanding his attention entranced Joe.

"Joe Richards, may I introduce Bint Nefsoud our new dream-maker." Cindi smiled.

The mare's eyes shone large and luminous. Her nostrils expanded like the most delicate flowers. A slight breeze gently lifted the mare's fine silky mane. She was the most magnificent little mare that he had ever seen. She was breathtaking.

"She's yours?" he asked.

"Yes and she is carrying Fire Cracker's foal." The words hit him hard. He couldn't believe for a moment what he had heard. He looked at Cindi.

"What did you say?"

"It's true. The day that Fire Cracker died, I bred this mare AI. She is carrying his last foal, and the foal will be yours, Joe." He stared at Cindi.

"You're not kidding, are you?"

"Not at all," Cindi laughed.

"Why would you do that for me?"

"It's a good thing to do. You deserve it. I can afford to do it. All of the above, plus I really want to. There could be a few stumbling blocks, though. Your dad mentioned an agreement that the syndicate had requested he sign about gelding Fire Cracker, should he return home."

"How could they demand anything after the way they treated him," he said immediately furious.

"Well I think that if there is a problem getting this foal registered it will come from the syndication. I don't want you to worry about this problem for one minute. It will be taken care of by and by." She winked at him. "This mare is Bedouin. She's very rear and is eighteen years young this year. She has taken very well to this pregnancy.

"Yes," Joe agreed, "she looks half her age."

"The foal is a gift from Fire Cracker and a gift from Bint and I," she smiled. Right now I need to check on our burgers or we could have charcoal." She touched his arm.

"I'll be along," Joe said. "I want a minute to let this sink in."

"I know, I know," Cindi waved. You come along when you're ready."

The mare nosed Joe's hand that he had on the top rail of the fence. Soft warm breaths blew across his skin. The mare appeared wise. Her eyes held the knowledge of all there was to know and all that had ever been. Denneyse suddenly was beside him.

"Isn't she wonderful?" she breathed.

"Much more than wonderful, " Joe agreed.

"She'll be nineteen when she foals. She doesn't look it at all.

"No not at all," Joe said.

"Cindi has guarded over her since she bought her as a five year old."

"You know I didn't know doc even owned an Arabian," Joe said.

"She's not partial to any one kind of horse, but this lady is her favorite," Denneyse smiled.

"Hey, you all," came the shout.

"I was supposed to retrieve you. Cindi knew you wouldn't want to leave the mare."

"She sees me over here with two terrific girls, now I'm supposed to eat?" he protested.

"Well as to eating, that's up to you." Dennyse laughed. Even her eyes smiled at him and they began the walk to the picnic tables.

CHAPTER 5

Maybe it was the weather, but as he stepped out on the half-finished deck of his cabin and felt the cool fall breeze, he suddenly had the urge to explore the countryside. He drove slowly. He'd waved two cars around him as he alternately looked at the forest and the road and drove generally south, southwest along the national forest boundary.

After about a mile, he pulled off to the side of the highway and parked. He sat in the truck for a moment getting his bearings looking up through the forest. The trees were a mixture of native pines and hardwood, oak and hickory, maples, and ash, and they were now shades of gold and red from a recent frost. A trickle of a spring came from the bank on his right, and Joe imagined his property somewhere over the top of the rise.

He got out of his truck and began the hike up the hill. He wanted to discover the possibility of an access to the forestry property from his land, hopefully a scenic trail good enough to ride a horse through. His hike turned into a beautiful walk as he wound his way through the bramble along the bottom by the highway and then broke into the high native forest above.

About a mile in, the trees opened up and another creek joined the small one he had been following, then turned right in the direction of his property. He continued walking beside it.

The stream grew wider with slick gray granite boulders beneath the surface of the clear water. Native grasses along the bank were bent over from the cold fall rains. Blue Jays darted among the tall trees, scolding his presence in their sanctuary. Joe looked around him in awe. What a lovely spot he had found. Sounds of water falling filled the forest. Hopping from boulder to boulder, he crossed the stream following the sound that seemed to be coming from the other side of a low ridge on his left. Walking up the ridge, he heard lots of water splashing somewhere below him. It could be heard clearly. He started down the bank, jumping sideways to keep from sliding on the slick bank.

Around a stand of huge trees, the prettiest waterfall he'd ever seen magically appeared. He sunk down on his haunches on the bank and watched it cascade happily over the layers of charcoal-colored granite. The stream fell ten or twelve feet into a pool at the bottom of the waterfall where a sandy beach surrounded a promising swimming hole. Completely mesmerized by the scene, he sat there on the bank at least thirty minutes before he realized that his land would be very close to this place, and he rose and headed down stream. Ten minutes later, the stream entered his little meadow and he was home. "Well, I'll be," he said. The waterfall was behind his property. The very same creek ran through his meadow.

Later, he would discover that the waterfall he found was Wildcat Branch Falls, and he was hugely disappointed that he wasn't the great white explorer of new lands that he had thought. He visited the falls often over the winter months, watching nature change the fall colors to the colors of winter, and then back to the colors of spring with its abundant wild flowers of blue, yellow and purple. He planned to ride Bint to this very place after her foal came, since he had never seen anyone in the area and the forest floor was clear of brush. It promised to be a safe place for a foal to tag along. The discovery of his special place in the foothills of the Blue Ridge Mountains gave him the sanctuary he needed from the great corporate beast, MCI. He'd been at MCI six months. During that time he was often reminded of the layers of authority within the corporation that he had to wade through. The simple structure of the forest and nature gave him the sense of peace that he craved. Sadly, during the passing year at MCI, Joe found that his busy job did not leave him time for things he loved. He pushed thoughts away of being cheated by time that continued to plague him. Those thoughts plagued him, despite his efforts.

He was sitting on a concrete block in front of his unfinished log cabin watching Bint lumber about in her paddock. The sun was disappearing behind the Blue Ridge Mountains. By noon, he found the mare was dripping milk from her utter. Her time was very near.

Joe had constructed two stalls and a feed room with a walkway between. One stall was sixteen-by-sixteen. That was the stall in which Bint would foal. The other stall was twelve-by-twelve. It was a tiny barn compared to his dad's at the ranch, but it was safe and roomy. There were two paddocks, one for each stall, giving him the option of turning the horse out, or closing the horse in the barn area. He liked this arrangement. It had proven convenient when he had to go to work. Joe got up and walked into the paddock where Bint stood resting with her head hung low.

"How you doin' lady?' he asked the mare. "Good girl," he murmured rubbing her shoulder. He peeked beneath the horse's abdomen. Joe led her in to her stall, checked to see that she had plenty of water, and latched the doors. He quietly left the stall. "Going for a sandwich Bint," he said. "Be back directly." And he went to the house.

Joe checked the mare twice. On the second visit at four in the morning, the horse had begun pacing the perimeter of her stall. Joe clicked on an old am/fm radio that he played in the barn. He was a firm believer that country western music soothed the horse. If he was wrong he figured at least it soothed him. The vision of his dad snoring contently in the hayloft passed through his mind. He missed his father. He was leaning against the wall of the stall watching the mare. How many times had he done this, he wondered. Now he had the opportunity to watch the last Fire Cracker foal come into the world, and he was hoping, for all he was worth, that this new foal would fill the empty spaces that the passing of Fire Cracker had left in his heart. Joe yawned and checked his watch. It was 5:05 a.m. Daylight came early in April. With a sudden spin, the mare turned and went down on the wheat straw bedding. She rolled onto her side. Joe grimaced, then smiled suddenly at the sudden return of the same old feelings of nervousness that foaling caused him. Some things did not change.

Bint Nefsoud stretched sideways, rolled up slightly, then groaned as she exhaled. She flipped her tail over her back. As he watched her labor progress, his mind was running through names that he had thought of and written down on a sheet of paper after he had researched Bint's bloodlines. What he had learned was that Hadban by Rodania had given the Arab world the incomparable Nefisa, the dam of twenty-one foals, one of whom was the spectacular foundation mare Bint Nefsoud, who was foaling right before his eyes this very moment. He recalled Mesoud, one of the founders of modern American breeding producing the dam of Nafia and Nax, foundress of the mare family responsible for the building of the great mare lines in early American endurance racing, including Naseel, dam of the great stallion—Hashaba. Berk by Naseel gave America Hashaba. Berk was imported through Ali Pasha Sherif himself. Hashaba was Fire Cracker's sire, this foal's grand sire. Fire Cracker—he thought to himself, how he missed their times together. Suddenly the mare stood, grabbing his attention. She was bathed in sweat as she whirled again and went down.

"Huh oh," Joe puffed out his cheeks and blew. Beads of perspiration lined his brow. He stepped quietly into the stall with the mare. He knew that Bint did not have the luxury of time. The third stage of labor was critical. Joe got down on his knees behind the mare. He continued talking to her. "Good girl. I'm here. It's ok, now let's get this little one." The mare knew he was there. Her right eye was focused toward him. He slipped on his long plastic gloves. The mare straightened her hind legs and pushed. Joe saw a tiny white hoof. Then, as the mare stopped pushing, the hoof disappeared.

"Darn," he said. "One more time gal, come on now." The mare's legs tensed again. There was the hoof. Joe slid his right hand into the mare searching for the other hoof. It was there, right along with a tiny nose. "Good–good," he exhaled in relief. "Now again," he said, knowing full well the mare either would or would not do as he prayed. As if she felt his tension, the mare bore down again. "A little more," Joe whispered. "Good, by golly," he exclaimed, "but this is a big foal. No wonder we're struck." Joe got a good hold then, and closed his big fist over two small hooves. He pulled down, tugging the foal, pulling him down, following along the curvature of the mare's spine. There was a sucking sound, then the colt's head, front feet and wide shoulders popped into view. "We got him now," he smiled. Joe tore the thin white sack covering the foal and it broke in a rush of wet. The dark head poked up, little tippy ears bent in opposite directions sticking straight out. A nose splashed with white extended, and the foal nickered. The morning sun streaked through the slats of the door. Joe suddenly realized that there were other sounds around him, and Willie Nelson sang 'Good Morning America, How Are You? Don't You Know Me, I'm your Native Son?'

"It's a beautiful colt," Joe sighed resting on his heels. He was born to the tune that Willie Nelson made famous, 'Good Morning America How Are You?' The bay colt with a splash of white on his face and four white socks, came out of the lovely mare Bint Nefsoud by the stallion Fire Cracker. "Lordy girl you have outdone yourself this time." Joe grinned. 'I'll Be Gone 500 Miles when The Day is Done,' Willie sang. "I sure hope so," Joe began singing along with the song.

"America," Joe repeated. All the names he had studied over, labored over and chosen particularly trying to keep to the bloodlines of the sire and the dam fell away as Willie belted out, 'Good Morning America How Are You?'

"It's America," he said to the colt as he rubbed him with the towel.

CHAPTER 6

"You know, regrets are like hangnails. They keep on aggravating you, until you just get shed of them." Clyde snapped his finger and thumb together. He was making coffee in his big sunny kitchen. Susan was half listening and making a list of supplies that Clyde was supposed to pick up the next day on his trip to Greenville.

"Yep, I guess so," she agreed. "I don't have regrets myself. I've been fortunate to be able to do just about what I please."

"Well, we both know that," Clyde said. "You are a hard-headed and obstinate woman."

"Look, don't be lavish in your compliments, Clyde," she looked up.

He continued on, "All those years of raising those beautiful animals and I never once got to ride one in that endurance ride in California, the Tevis race."

"Umm, I've heard of that ride, looks dangerous. Especially for a man your age Clyde."

"Only thing that counts is the trust that the horse has in you and the trust that you have in it," he continued. The smell of fresh coffee was filling the room.

"Maybe I will have that cup," Susan said. "How about toilet paper Clyde, you have enough of that?"

"You know, woman, you have a way of intruding on a body's dreams."

"Yeah," she smiled. "I've been told that a time or two."

"That Tevis ride," he shook his head, "what I wouldn't give to ride that." He sighed. "That's my regret, that and not being able to talk you into being my wife."

"Well, Clyde, that's not so bad, only two regrets."

"I guess not," he conceded. He didn't mention that the Tevis ride regret was harder to live with than the marrying regret.

The Tevis ride stewed around in his old brain all the next week. He thought seriously that he might be addled. The Arabian registry logo kept popping into his head. 'Want to Ride? Really ride?' Clyde loved to ride. His heroes had always been cowboys, just like the song. Just to humor himself he wrote off to the Arabian registry and asked questions about the Tevis ride; after all he was only sixty.

Joe picked up the ringing telephone. "Joe, this is Susan. Your dad is off on one of his adventures, I'm afraid."

"What's up Susan?"

"Well, he left this morning and wanted me to call you. He's on his way to New York State to buy a filly."

"I thought he was out of the horse business?"

"Well I think he means to train this filly and enter her in the Tevis cup in California. Now, I may be jumping to conclusions here because he didn't really tell me that, but he's been talking about the Tevis race for quite some time now."

"You've got to be kidding."

"Not when it comes to Clyde Richards I'm not kidding."

"Great—He's the one that talked me into taking Baz and America to the state fair to show America in the Go-

As-You-Please class, and now he's on his way to New York? Go figure," Joe said.

"Joe—he arranged for Denneyse to come help you this morning. She's probably on her way by now. Anyway, I'm following orders to call and let you know darlin'," Susan said. She was grinning into the receiver.

"You're telling me that Denneyse Danner is on the way to my house?"

"As we speak," she said.

"Great, great let me go then, thanks Susan." He didn't have time to worry about his dad's nutty ideas. Clyde wouldn't let go of the matchmaking. Joe moved through the house ripping off his dirty tee shirt and pants, hopping on one leg, then the other, throwing clothes on the bedroom floor. He stepped into the shower grumbling. He stepped out of the shower and was still grumbling when the doorbell rang. He pulled on his old gym shorts and ran to the door, still rubbing his sandy blond hair.

"Hi," he said. "Sorry I didn't know you were coming out."

"That's ok," she laughed. A fresh soapy smell filled the doorway.

"Oh sorry, come on in." Joe stepped aside. He thought he was beginning to sound like a kid in high school. "Let me get dressed. Won't take a minute," he said already walking away.

"Take your time, really. I know this is a surprise. It was a surprise to me too."

"It was?"

"Yep," she grinned.

"My dad." He made a face and disappeared into the bedroom again. "Seems he's on mission." She watched his muscular back disappear around the corner. Get a grip, she whispered to herself. Then she looked down at her worn jeans. He'll think I don't own anything but old faded jeans. But she figured she would be helping with America and would be horsy soon anyway.

"Yes, I heard. Your dad is something else," she laughed.

"Make yourself at home," he hollered over his shoulder on the way into the bathroom to shave.

She stepped into the cute little kitchen and stood in front of the sink. Looking out the window she could see the Blue Ridge Mountain foothills. "Great view," she yelled at Joe. Then she drew a glass of water from the tap. The water was cold and sweet. "Great water too," she said. "This is such a terrific place Joe, you're so lucky," she hollered. He was standing behind her.

"I really like it," he said softly. She jumped. He laughed again.

"Didn't mean to scare you."

"Your climbing rose on the banister of the porch is such a beautiful pink."

"It was a cutting from my mother's rose bush at the ranch. I planted it and it really took off."

"Well, it's gorgeous," she smiled.

"We better get moving," he said. "We have two hours, but I don't like to get to a show late. You never know what can hold you up," he said.

Joe led Bint into the three-horse slant load trailer. He had removed all of the dividers to safely haul the colt and his dam. He attached Bint's halter to the quick release by the front window. America was supposed to follow nicely into the trailer behind his dam. Well, that didn't work. Denneyse was struggling to hold the colt still. He was walking on his hind legs and dancing around. He whinnied indignantly that his dam dare walk off and leave him behind. Bint nickered to him. Joe moved out of the trailer, put his arm behind the colt's brown fuzzy butt, and heaved him forward. America's front feet planted stubbornly in the dirt, but the colt slid forward, and as he came to the step up he lifted both front legs at the same time and leaped like a deer into the trailer. Denneyse laughed.

"Well, he can jump."

"Yep." Joe agreed and closed the heavy door. They were off.

Driving down the freeway, they settled into easy conversation about Clemson University. Then Denneyse said, "How are you going to show him?" She was looking out the side window, watching as they rushed past all of the green fields.

"Well do you have any ideas? What would be the best way?"

She looked at Joe thoughtfully. "I would, if it were me, that is, leave Bint in her stall and take him into the arena. If it's his first time he'll be so excited about Bint not being there he should really strut his stuff. Besides, he leads well enough that you can handle him. He'll be so excited that everyone will fall in love with him instantly. That's what I think." She said and went back to the landscape flowing by.

"You do huh?" Joe looked at her profile. Her face was lean with prominent cheekbones straight nose and full lips. The wind whipped her ponytail wildly.

"Ok, we'll try it," he agreed.

She turned her face toward him. "Yeah?" she asked. He nodded and she smiled.

True to Denneyse's word, America entered the class strutting like a park horse, four white feet flashing. His little fuzzy tail flagged straight in the air and he called his heart out for his mother to save him. The folks in the bleachers only had eyes for him. Much to the dismay of a lot of amateur contestants, America stole the show and took his first blue ribbon. Joe and Denneyse were delighted. They chattered about their strategy on the way home.

"You're a natural as a show consultant Denneyse," he told her. "I may need your expertise again."

"Anytime," she smiled, "my fees are nominal." She laughed, but her instincts told her that it was a very good excuse to get back to the little farm in the foothills again.

"Mornin' Joe." It was Clyde on the other end of the phone line.

"Hey dad, you're back in town?" The phone rang early if Clyde was calling.

"Yep. Sorry I missed America's first show, son. I know, I was supposed to help you and all, but, well, I figured Denneyse would make a pretty good substitute for an old man, especially if the old man is your dad." Joe knew that Clyde was well pleased with his slick maneuver. He just rolled his eyes and didn't give him the satisfaction of a comment.

"Can you believe first place? That was all because of Denneyse's idea about leaving Baz in her stall and taking America out alone. He was in a mighty tizzy without his momma. A guy called me the very next day and offered me $5,000 for him as soon as he's weaned."

"I'm not surprised. He's a heck of a nice colt. You'll be getting a lot of calls for that colt as time goes on. Question is, will they offer you enough to pry him loose?"

"Never," Joe laughed.

"Not to change the subject, son."

"That means you're going to, but go ahead," Joe laughed.

"I want you to come look at what I brought home."

"Which is?" Joe asked.

"Just the best filly I've ever seen son. You know that Basey Tankersley out west?"

"Sure who doesn't?"

"Well this filly is by one of her best studs and out of a mare that was imported from a sale in Egypt about five years ago. This filly's dam was bought for 3.5 million. A tidy sum."

"Yeah—but what is she worth in today's market, dad?"

"Well, the quality is all I cared about anyway. I mean to ride her in the Tevis cup one day."

"You do—do you?"

"Sure do."

"How old is this filly?"

"She's right for you to break," Clyde said happily.

"Me. You expect me to break her?"

"You didn't expect to put an old man up on her did you," Clyde asked.

"My point exactly, if she's wild and young, what in the world are you doing buying her for yourself?" Joe asked. "Never mind, I expect I'd better come take a look. I need to see what you've gotten me into I guess."

"Reckon so," Clyde agreed. "Come on then."

Later that afternoon Joe and Clyde were standing on the bottom rail of the round pen at the ranch in Camden. Clyde was rolling his toothpick around in his mouth thoughtfully, and Joe reached up and pulled his Clemson baseball cap lower on his forehead.

"She's black," Joe said, "Blue black, not a touch of white anywhere." The filly was prancing and dancing, blowing and snorting. She kicked three successive times at the round pen wall. The motions were so quick that they were a blur. She was fire in motion. The round pen was shady, and the sun glittered off her black satin coat as it filtered through the oak leaves. She was stunning. "Good thing you made this round pen out of telephone poles," he commented. Clyde shifted his toothpick to the other side. "Well I already knew she was black and I admit she's a little feisty," Clyde shrugged.

"Feisty. You call that feisty. I'm just hoping she's not completely nuts. How in the heck did you manage to get her in the horse trailer?"

"Well, now, that old boy was raising cows too. So they just ran her down the cow chute and into my trailer. She was ok once she got in there. I had a little grain and hay for here. She only kicked the back door a couple of times. You know I got it padded with that old rubber matting, so it was fine. I can't expect any better behavior. Shoot, they just weaned her off her mama and threw her out with the other weanlings. There was a herd of twenty-five fillies; she's the best one of the bunch, I'll tell you. This mare is by that stallion Silver Ghost and a chestnut mare name of Baz." Baz? Joe was thinking, but he said, "Black out of gray and chestnut and she's desert bred." Clyde was well aware of her breeding and her potential. He just wasn't going to say any 'I told you so's' until he was certain she wasn't part fire dragon.

"Well she has the body all right," Joe conceded. "But getting a handle on her might prove to be a real job."

"Yeah, but I figured I had the man for the job," Clyde grinned.

"Just a thought here, dad. If she's for you, why pick one that hasn't been touched?"

"Well, now, that's as plain as day, son. She ain't been messed up neither."

His dad had a way of simplifying everything.

"I guess we'll see then," Joe said.

"Yep—that's what I say," Clyde agreed.

CHAPTER 7

During the month of July 1988, Joe sent America's application of registration in to the Arabian Horse Registry in Fort Collins, Colorado. September 1988 he received the Subpoena.

He could not believe what he was reading:

Order to appear before the honorable Judge Judith Helms, October 27, 1988, City of Los Angeles, Los Angeles County California at 9 a.m. regarding the ownership of the Arabian Stallion (Pending Registration #868534), prodigy of the Arabian stallion, Fire Cracker registration #463086 owned by Suwalli Enterprises, deceased at the date of prodigy's birth. These charges have been duly filed in county court this day, October 3, 1988 by Jack McDonald, representative and attorney of Suwalli Enterprises, against plaintiff, hereinafter referred to as Richards' Arabians and Joseph Richards, applicant for registration of the stallion America #868534, (pending).

Suwalli Enterprises is charging fraudulent claims of ownership to the above named stallion, America. Failure to appear in court on the appointed date will result in abandonment of all further rights to and relinquishment of ownership by one Joseph Richards, Richards' Arabians Camden, and South Carolina.

"That's all it says," Joe told Doctor Cindi Arters. "I have to appear and plead my case or I lose him."

"You're not going to lose him. That is just not going to happen, Joe. Have you called your father yet?"

"No, I have only called you."

"Ok. Let me make the calls, including the one to your father. I'll get back to you. If we're lucky we'll send them to jail."

Joe couldn't bear the thought of losing America. He had expected a fight over the colt's registration. He had no idea it could mean losing him all together. Fear rose in his gut. This just could not happen again.

The next day Clyde was on the telephone.

"May I speak to Doctor Glen Eubanks, please?" Clyde asked politely. A woman had answered the phone on the fifth ring. She had a small voice.

"No," she said softly. "Doctor Eubanks passed away this past June."

"Oh, no," Clyde said. "I'm so sorry, miss. Did the doctor have a wife?"

"May I ask who's calling please?" she asked.

"Sure, I'm sorry. My name is Clyde Richards. Let me tell you why I'm calling. Way back in August of '86 I came through Redlands with an Arabian stallion in tow. I sold him to a syndicate in Oakland and they didn't treat him good. He was repeatedly injured while he was in their care. The doctor was good enough to see him on my trip home. He treated him and then took a lot of pictures and told me to call him if I needed his help. Well, we sure do need his help. My stallion passed away after I got him home, but not before my vet got a donation from the old boy. Now we have a great colt by that stallion. But the syndication people are fighting us on getting the colt registered.

They have filed a law suit and are trying to get the colt from us. We have to go to court in October. We need all the help we can get. I thought Dr. Eubanks' pictures would truly help us out."

"I'm Mrs. Eubanks, Mr. Richards."

"I'm sorry to hear of your misfortune, Ms. Eubanks," Clyde said. "I lost my wife many years ago and I understand what a hard thing it is."

"Yes, Mr. Richards, it is. Glen was a wonderful man; I didn't have near enough time with him. But let's see...Glen kept a lot of information for people, papers and pictures. I promise I will go through all of his files and see if I can locate your pictures for you. Please give me your phone number and address again just in case, she said. I know that Glen would want to help you very much. He lived for his animals."

Clyde hung up the telephone. They really needed those pictures, he realized. If a vet in California could back up their local vet, they would be a lot less likely to have to put up with any shenanigans from the likes of Suwalli.

Several weeks later at nine in the evening Clyde's telephone rang.

"Mr. Richards?" came the soft voice.

"This is Clyde Richards," he held his breath.

"We're in luck sir. I have found your pictures. Glen had them tucked away in a manila envelope all ready for mailing. Your address was missing on it. It looked as though he'd lost your address. The stamps were already on the envelope." Clyde had almost given up on the pictures. This surely was a good omen, he thought.

"Shall I send them on to you today then?" she asked.

"If you would be so kind, missus, send them overnight to me. We are flying out Thursday for the hearing. So you see, we haven't much time."

"Ok, I will surely do that for you."

"I'll reimburse you the cost for the overnight mail, missus."

"No, no, that won't be necessary. I am doing just fine. One thing that Glen believed in was insurance."

"Then I would like to make a donation to a charity in his name," Clyde insisted.

"That would be wonderful Mr. Richards. He was partial to the Federation for Abused Animals here in Redlands. Let's see, I'll get the address. I had it right here on their newsletter. Yes, here it is. It is 1009 Center Street, Redlands, California 92373. I hope the pictures help you. His notes will be in the package too. Please let me know how this works out, will you?"

"Sure will. My best to you." Clyde smiled.

True to her word, Clyde's overnight package arrived the next afternoon. There were eight photos taken close up. Five showed the old wounds that had healed over. The other three were recent. The most damaging had been under Fire Cracker's girth area. The wound in the picture was an elongated rip deep enough to emit fluid and was obviously infected. Dr. Eubanks' opinion clearly stated that the horse had reared and come down on an object hard enough to cause internal damage. The wound had not been treated before his treatment. His assessment of the abuse and malnourishment took five typewritten pages. The doctor was of the opinion that the neglect had taken place over a long period of time. The doctor had the foresight to have his signature notarized and copies of his licenses and degrees attached. Here was the work of a man used to dealing with trouble. Clyde was ecstatic. This certainly would help their case and help get America's registration in order.

CHAPTER 8

Joe moved Georgee Girl to his place for training, and the new occupant in the barn seemed quite interesting to Bint and America. He started his routine with Georgee immediately.

Joe approached her stall, slid the bar and stepped in. The mare ran to the far corner and turned to face him. "No, I didn't come for a fight, girl," he said softly. The mare began pawing the ground. "Just comin' to get acquainted. You'll be seeing lots of me for a while. At least until you figure out I'm an ok guy and we can be friends." America was listening to Joe's voice in the stall across the walkway and whinnied. "That's right, see he knows all this stuff and he's just a little guy. He knows I'm an ok guy. I'll just move around in here and you'll see I'm a good guy." Joe began walking to his right slowly, and the filly moved off in the other direction. Then he turned and doubled back. Georgee stopped, faced him, and blew. "Well, I know you don't understand, but you will and as soon as you start coming to me, I'll leave you in peace," he said softly.

"Now I'll pretend I don't see you and I'll just walk away." The filly watched him and took one step in his direction. "That was real good," he told her. "Now I'll just stand here and move this straw around. 'Course you won't understand that either, but it won't hurt you, will it?" The filly watched Joe, then in a moment she reached for a bite of her hay. "Well, isn't that something. I'm already boring to you right? It's ok to go on and eat with me here, isn't it Georgee?" Joe walked straight toward the filly. She had both eyes on him but straight on vision in a horse isn't as good as side vision, and before she knew it, he was in front of her. Her eyes were wide and she was trembling.

"It's ok girl, I'm not going to hurt you. I don't want to touch you today. I'm going to go away now, you watch," Joe smiled and stepped back then slowly moved away from her. He stood by the stall door a few minutes talking to her all the time. Then he stepped quietly out of her stall. "Ok, Georgee, that wasn't bad. I'll come back to talk to you this evening girl," he said. He looked in on America before he left the barn and then went to work. He felt satisfied that the first introduction went quietly, considering the filly didn't know anything about people.

At the end of the week Clyde came up for a visit. He found Joe sitting above his new round pen on a big wooden bench observing Georgee Girl. He was sitting on a bench that he had made for this very spot. He built it because he knew that Clyde loved to sit and watch a horse. Clyde had been known to study a horse for hours on end. Clyde appeared after his twenty-minute nap and knew exactly where to find him.

Watching Georgee, Joe admitted to himself that once he got past her beauty, the filly had extremely nice conformation. Of course, his dad had a very good eye for horseflesh. That's how they had stayed in business in Camden for so many years. The filly began to canter around the pen. She was moving slow, working from her rear, and rolling gently along at a comfortable speed. She wasn't storming ahead like she did when Clyde had first brought her home. Clyde walked up behind him. It was coming on to evening and the cicadas were beginning their songs. The day's heat was leaving the baked soil. The sun was diving for the west. It was Clyde's favorite time of day. A gathering time, Clyde called it. It was a time to gather thoughts and recount what had been accomplished. It was a peaceful time to sit and watch the day end while watching a beautiful horse romp and play.

"Ahh these are the things that make for a good life," Clyde said as he sat down. He was missing his Peggy. He wished she could see all of this. He wished she could see how well their son had grown. Maybe she can see it, he thought. "How's my horse doin'?"

"Not bad. I sacked her out with an old burlap bag yesterday and today," Joe replied, looking at the filly.

"Yeah, well, what happened today, cause I can imagine what happened yesterday."

"Actually," Joe shrugged, "she jumped out a little yesterday, but surprisingly she didn't do much of anything today."

"Ha, she's smart ain't she?" Clyde said. "Maybe I picked a good horse then."

"Maybe. I'm not ready to go that far yet. By next week if I'm not in a body cast, we'll know for sure you picked a smart horse."

"I got the right trainer too," Clyde laughed.

"Well, the price is pretty good," Joe said. Clyde looked at him.

"Time you're on her back—you'll be beggin' to pay me." Clyde grinned. Joe just shook his head. "You'll see, she's a war horse. She ain't afraid of nothing or nobody,"

Clyde rolled his toothpick over in his teeth. "By the way, not to change the subject."

Clyde leaned back against the back of the bench so he could watch Joe's face. "How's Denneyse been?" Boy he doesn't give up, Joe thought.

"Good," Joe said. He didn't move a muscle in his face. He was well aware of his dad's famous observations.

"You all see much of each other?"

"Some," Joe said.

"Some. Now what kind of an answer is that?"

"Just some is all," Joe smiled. "I'm seeing her, we're dating, ok? That's it. We're busy. We have jobs and now we're training horses, plural. Because—as if I didn't have enough to train with America, who will be the Tevis cup winner in several years. Now I'm training my fathers' wild horse so he can challenge me his son, in the Tevis Race. I do believe this was a conspiracy on your part dad. I haven't determined what kind."

"Well now you don't have to get so excited," Clyde said. "I just thought I'd sit a spell and watch the day end and see how life was treating you and my new horse is all."

"We're working on it dad."

"That's good son. That's the best we can do. I'll see you tomorrow evening, then, after work."

"Can't tomorrow dad. I'm taking Denneyse over to Spartenburg to a clinic that we wanted to go to."

"Oh? Well I'll see you when you're not so busy." Clyde chuckled all the way to the house. He liked that Joe got antsy about the girl. Meant he didn't want him prying. "That's real good," he said to himself.

October 27, 1988 Circuit Court Judge Judith Helms, County of Los Angeles, Los Angeles County Court House, Los Angeles, California 9 a.m.

"This court is called to order. Judge Judith Tucker Helms presiding. Please rise," the clerk of the court called out. Judge Judith Helms entered the courtroom, and stood for facing the courtroom and said, "Please be seated." Everyone sat.

The clerk began reading: "The complaint is based on charges filed in the county court regarding the theft on one Arabian stallion, Fire Cracker, registration #463086, removed from the premises of Suwalli Enterprises on or about April 15, 1986, highway 680, Oakland, California. Opening statement from the plaintiff given by Suwalli Enterprises attorney Jack McDonald: The plaintiff has testified that there was a verbal agreement between the seller and Mr. Clyde Richards that upon the reclamation of said stallion, Fire Cracker, the horse was to be castrated."

"Objection your honor," Clyde's attorney, Bill Anderson stood. "There was no such agreement your honor, either verbal or written. This statement, therefore, is hearsay."

"Mr. McDonald, are you ready to present written proof about this agreement?" the judge asked.

"Your honor, Suwalli Enterprises can prove that Mr. Richards was aware of the agreement, and since our claims are based upon this agreement, we would like the opportunity to show that Mr. Richards acted flagrantly with only his best interest at heart."

"May I remind the plaintiff that being aware of an agreement and actually having one is different."

"Yes your honor," Jack McDonald agreed.

"What was that all about?" Joe asked Bill Anderson.

"I think the judge is getting ticked." Bill whispered.

The clerk requested the opening statement from the defendant's attorney, Bill Anderson, for his clients Joseph and Clyde Richards of Richards' Arabians, Camden, South Carolina.

"Your honor, the defense will prove three things today. We concur that yes, Suwalli Enterprises proposed the agreement to which Mr. McDonald refers. We intend to prove that: #1. Mr. Clyde Richards refused the agreement. #2. That Suwalli Enterprises fully intended to default on the agreement to pay in full the balance owed on the horses acquired from my client Clyde Richards of Richards' Arabians, and finally, #3. That my client removed the stallion Fire Cracker from Suwalli Enterprises premises for the safety and well being of the horse, putting himself in grave danger in the process."

The courtroom was silent. Judge Judy looked up over her eye glasses to the plaintiff's counselor and said: "Precede then, Mr. McDonald. We need to settle this in a timely manner."

"Yes your honor." Jack McDonald looked a tad sheepish.

Clyde was smiling. It sounded to him like they just made a base hit. He retrieved a toothpick from the inside pocket of his corduroy jacket and resettled in his chair. His Stetson was lying on the table next to him.

"Court calls Mr. Clyde Richards to the stand." Bill Anderson followed behind his client to the front of the courtroom.

At 6'2" gray wavy hair and brilliant blue eyes, Clyde presented an appearance of someone to reckon with, even at the age of sixty. He walked confidently with a long strong stride to the chair he was to sit in and turned to face the courtroom. He removed his toothpick. His Stetson was in his left hand. He raised his right hand to be sworn in.

"Mr. Richards, you sold Fire Cracker to Suwalli Enterprises in 1982?"

"Yes."

"Suwalli signed a contract with you agreeing to pay $200,000 in five installments to Richards' Arabians, is that correct?"

"Yes."

"Did they pay you five installments of $200,000?"

"No sir, they paid four installments and went belly up."

"Meaning bankrupt?"

"Yes sir, that's what I mean."

"Your honor, this is a copy of the contract in question." Bill Anderson handed a copy of the contract to the court clerk.

"Approximately two weeks before the last payment you were to receive, you had a phone call from Mr. McDonald, is that correct sir?"

"Yes sir, that's correct." Clyde agreed.

"In this phone conversation, Mr. McDonald said that Suwalli had filed for bankruptcy, and that in lieu of your last payment, Fire Cracker was to be auctioned off to the highest bidder, is that correct sir?"

"That's what Jack McDonald said, yes."

"When you protested and told Jack McDonald you wanted your horse back, what did Mr. McDonald tell you?"

"He said they had thought of that. He said if I wanted him back that was ok, but I had to sign this agreement to have Fire Cracker castrated." Clyde stared directly at Jack McDonald.

"What did you tell Mr. McDonald when he said that Clyde?"

"I told him over my dead body. I told him that they owed me another $200,000 and if they were rescinding their agreement, I sure didn't feel I had to agree to anything that they wanted." There was a stir in the courtroom. People everywhere in the courtroom had their heads bobbing up and down.

"Ok, Clyde, what happened then?"

"Well, McDonald told me that if I didn't sign the agreement, they were going ahead with the plan to auction Fire Cracker on April 15, 1986. He said he would send me whatever they received at the auction in lieu of the contract price."

"I see. This must have upset you, Mr. Richards."

"There hasn't been a day I haven't regretted selling that horse. When McDonald told me they were going to auction him to the highest bidder, I just couldn't let that happen."

"Ok, Mr. Richards, what exactly did you do after your conversation with Mr. McDonald?"

"I threw my belongings into my truck, checked my wallet, hooked up my horse trailer, made a phone call, and went to California." Laughter broke out in the back rows of the room.

"I see, and you picked up your horse. What condition was your horse in Mr. Richards?"

"Objection. The last statement assumes ownership," Mr. McDonald said.

"Overruled." The judge frowned at McDonald. Clyde and Joe smiled at the same instant.

"You also have proof of mistreatment, don't you, Mr. Richards?" Bill Anderson asked.

"Well, I brought pictures with written opinions of two very well known veterinarians, sir," Clyde offered.

McDonald and one of his clients, Lloyd Sims, looked at one another. They were whispering.

Bill Anderson walked to the table and picked up an envelope.

"Please accept this envelope and its contents as evidence, defendant's exhibit 2a, your honor." Bill Anderson brought the folder with pictures of Fire Cracker, taken by Dr. Eubanks and Dr. Cindi Arters, forward.

"There will be a fifteen minute recess while I review this evidence. Court is adjourned." As the judge closed her chamber door, conversation broke out in the courtroom.

Judge Judith Helms promptly returned with quiet authority.

"Gentlemen, after reviewing the evidence of exhibit 2a, it is the opinion of this court that Suwallii Enterprises should never have had in their charge any animal, let alone one of such high value. What happened to Richards' Arabians was a travesty beyond understanding. It is my ruling that all claims pending against Richards' Arabians by Suwalli Enterprises be lifted, and claims that Suwalli Enterprises has regarding ownership of one Arabian Stallion, America #868534 (pending) are denied. However, there is one stumbling block, Mr. Richards. The court is going to request that you move forward in obtaining the blood typing that the Arabian Registry now requires for proof of parentage. If the stallion America is indeed Fire Cracker's progeny—then I see no reason for this court to stand in your way, and I, for one, wish you both the best of luck with this stallion. Court is adjourned gentlemen." With a flurry, Judge Judith Helms was suddenly gone and Clyde had really wanted to hug her.

CHAPTER 9

Joe was standing in the center of the round pen as America cantered the perimeter. He stepped forward with the lounge line as the horse came about. America immediately stopped his forward motion, rolled back over his hocks, and began cantering in the opposite direction.

"Wow," Denneyse said. "That was beautiful. You're a great trainer Joe." Joe smiled and kept the colt moving.

"Well it isn't so much about training the horse you see," he said slowly. America continued cantering easily around the pen. "See, this horse already knows how to do this stuff. He came into the world knowing how to canter and roll back over his hocks. He can do a sliding stop. He can jump a fence as high as his abilities will allow. He can walk and trot and do a flying change. He naturally circles on the correct leads. If you have ever watched a horse in the wild running with the herd, swerving this way and that, you will notice that the horse is never on the wrong lead. Think about it," he smiled. "The trick to all of this is getting the horse do these things when you want him to do them. So you might say I'm training myself to get the correct responses from this individual horse when I ask for them. Every horse is an individual, just like we are individuals. Some horses are just naturally mild-tempered. Some of them are grouchy. Some are arrogant, and some of them are just plain pissed off. But mostly, this horse is smarter than I am, unless I can figure out where he's coming from. I need to find what makes him tick, so to speak, and then if I'm real lucky he's going to let me look smarter than I am. I'm learning. This guy's a darn good teacher. I hope I'm a good pupil. He's got more moves than Mohamed Ali, D."

"I think so," she laughed. He had started calling her D once in a while. She liked it. He had even called her Dr. D on several occasions.

"It will be an honor riding this guy. He's classy and honest. He doesn't hedge on his movements. Watch him. His strides are powerful and confident. Man, he is really together." Joe's voice was full of excitement.

"Whoa," Joe said, and America slid to a stop and stood where he was. The stallion's nostrils flared and his coat was shiny with sweat.

"Step in," Joe called to the horse. America walked to him. The horse shook his head up and down.

"Yes, you were great," Joe said affectionately, and stroked the horse's powerful shoulder.

The first frost had come and gone the fall after America's second birthday. The weather turned warm again. It was an Indian summer. Joe looked to the paddock where America was grazing on late season grass and thought of climbing aboard that dark silky back. It would really be something, sitting on him, Joe mused. America had grown in all the right places. The horse was filled out everywhere. His hindquarters were round and well-muscled. His chest was broad and stout. At the age of 2 ½ he stood 15.1 hands tall. Joe thought it possible that he might grow a little more. The colt's legs were outstanding with the strong flat bone and well-defined tendons that the Arabs loved. He had beautiful wide, round hooves that were preferred among the Bedouins thousands of year ago. In short, he was the ideal Arabian. Joe hoped that America would be suited for the job he wanted him to do. He smiled at the thought. It was time to ride.

Joe started by biting the colt up in his stall every morning. He would detach the reins on the bridle and set him free so that the horse could adjust to the feel of the weight of the snaffle bit in his mouth.

The following week, Joe brought America to the round pen. The only problem Joe had was getting the young horse to walk away from him. It seemed Joe had a friend who didn't want to leave his side.

Next, Joe fitted a surcingle on him and attached long lines to it. The colt had a terrific attitude, and the lessons sped along so that on week three, Joe introduced America to the saddle. As Joe placed the saddle on America's, back the colt bent his neck and head around to smell the leather thing sitting on him.

"Yes you have to wear this thing," Joe smiled. "It makes it easier for me, not you. Good boy," he said after pulling the cinch up a little tighter. Then he asked America to canter with the saddle on. The colt did as he was asked. When Joe stopped him, he tightened the cinch a little more.

"Hey, how's it going with you all today?" Denneyse yelled as she was walking up.

"Your timing is impeccable. I was just thinking of riding this guy."

"Oh yeah? You're just going to buck him out?" she asked.

"This horse isn't going to buck," Joe laughed.

"Right," she said. "What colt doesn't buck?"

"This is a great colt, he won't buck, I'm telling you."

"Ok—I'll bet you," she grinned.

"Ok, what will we bet?"

"How about the dance Friday at the Barnyard in town. I've already bought the two tickets. You pay me for them if you lose. Deal?"

"Deal," he said.

"I'll have to meet you at the Barnyard, Friday is a late night at the clinic and it's a long drive up here."

"No problem." Joe smiled. "What better offer— a free dance with a pretty girl? Can't beat that."

Joe bent the colt's head around toward him and stepped up into the saddle.

"Wow," he said. It gave him goose bumps just being aboard the horse. America stood there.

"Well?" Denneyse asked. Joe pulled the left rein a little, asking the colt to step forward. America just stood there.

"Well?" she said again.

"Ok, ok. Give him a minute, he's thinking." Joe asked the same question of America, stronger this time. The colt suddenly squatted and leapt forward. They were off. Around the arena they flew. It was a race. Denneyse's eyes were wide, and her hand flew to her mouth.

Joe asked the horse for his head and said, "Whoa." America planted his front feet and stopped dead. Joe cut a flip and plopped right in front of the horse on his rear, reins still in hand. America shook his head and blew. Joe wondered if the horse was laughing at him.

"Thanks, big guy," Joe said to the colt.

"You know, you really did that well, Joe," Denneyse said. "I guess I'll have to pay for those tickets after all. He didn't buck, you were right." She laughed all the way back to her truck. Joe got off the ground brushing his backside.

"This is not the way we start, America. Let's try this one more time, maybe a little slower." The colt shook his head up and down. "Good boy," Joe agreed. "I'm sure we can come to some compromise."

CHAPTER 10

It was early February, and so far winter had amounted to nothing more than two weeks of cold rain and frost at night. Joe arrived at the ranch in Camden on a bright Saturday morning. Today they were going to ride.

He was tossing their saddles into the slant load trailer. "We're riding at the Camden Hunt Club this morning," he said over his shoulder as Denneyse walked up to him.

"Really?" she said, excited at the thought of going off somewhere new and riding. He went into the barn and came out with America.

"Georgee hasn't been loaded since I got her under saddle good," he said. "We'll just start today. Today will be Trailer Loading 101, the short course."

"Ok, if you say so," Denneyse wasn't convinced. But she was excited about the Hunt Club. She'd heard about it over and over. Now she was finally going.

"I pronounced Georgee trustworthy now. Let's see what she does when she gets a load of all that open space, creeks and ponds. You'll stick on, right?" He looked at Denneyse with raised eyebrows.

"Sure." She shrugged, then went into the barn for her horse. She came up to the back of the trailer leading the mare.

"Now don't stop walking," Joe said to her. "Stay at the mare's shoulder. Do not hesitate. She needs to think that this is an everyday occurrence. Lead her as if she has been doing it for ten years," Joe said. America was in his stall of the trailer waiting and he nickered as he heard Georgee approaching.

"Ok," Denneyse said, as she strode up to the back of the trailer, and she got one of her own feet in the trailer when Georgee stopped dead. At the same moment Joe was ready, and tapped the mare lightly on her left hip.

"Step up," he said to the mare loud and clear. The mare tentatively placed her right front foot into the trailer, then withdrew it again.

"Step up," Joe said, tapping her lightly again. This time the mare put both front feet in and Denneyse stepped all the way into the trailer with the mare as Joe continued tapping on the horse's hip. She was in.

Denneyse put the safety release lead on the mare and closed her door securely. Georgee immediately began blowing and munching her hay.

"Just like she'd done it ten years," Denneyse smiled as she exited the trailer.

Hunt clubs were originally for the wealthy to enjoy the sport of fox hunting in the South. They still did some fox hunting and held trials on occasion, complete with fox, dogs, horses and riders. The hunt club land was available to any equestrian for riding. There was over 5,000 acres in the Camden Hunt Club. The trails were in the forest through meadows and in the wide-open spaces. Camden Hunt Club offered the scenery and freedom as only a huge undeveloped piece of land can afford. There were jumps; trails galore, creeks and ponds all open to horseback riders. There were no motorized vehicles permitted and riders could enjoy the security of not having to look for cars on their ride. It was pure horse heaven. In the western United States there is federal land to play on. In the southeastern United States there is private land and hunt clubs.

Joe loved the Camden Hunt Club second only to the ranch.

As they rode along later this Saturday morning, coming up a rise from the first creek crossing, America and Georgee were prancing. The coolness of the morning good feed and a playful spirit had them pulling on the bit a little. Joe knew that America was ready for a run.

"How's she doing?" Joe asked Denneyse. They were trotting now; Georgee was several steps behind he and America.

"Great," Denneyse said breathlessly. "Oh, Joe, this is such a gorgeous place. I can't believe I haven't been coming here all along. I want to come here all the time. Is it all this fantastic?"

"Yep," he said. "Up over the rise there, we will be able to see the fire tower, and if we ride in that direction and then go to the left and down the hill a ways, we will come to the first black water pond."

"Black?" Denneyse asked, not sure she had heard correctly.

"That's what they call it. The pond water looks black when you're away from it. But when you get up close there is a white sand bottom and the water is crystal clear. We can take a swim if we can get your mule in the water," Joe laughed. "We will call it Going Into The Pond, lesson 101."

"Ok, let's go," she yelled.

At that, Joe pressed his heals into America's sides and the stallion leapt forward. She didn't have to tell Joe anything twice.

Pounding hooves echoed through the air. There were horses coming. Horses were coming, flying up the trail. Get out of the way fast. Quail, Bob White, Mocking birds flew for cover. Two little brown rabbits dove into the brush beside the trail. The only things that didn't move were the spiders that had painstakingly woven their webs from the trees along the trail, then crossed to the other side.

Shouts and laughing sounds came with the pounding of the hooves as they drew closer and closer.

"It got me," she screamed laughing. Joe urged America faster and faster. He was laughing so hard at Denneyse getting caught by all of the spider webs, that his sides were aching. He turned in the saddle, and showing off, threw his hands into the air. His reins were riding behind the saddle horn. Suddenly, a flash of orange on the side of the trail flashed by his peripheral vision—too late. America jumped sideways in full stride to avoid the orange object, and Joe went airborne. Puff! Dust flew and Denneyse barely missed hitting him and America as she turned and whirled Georgee around. Joe was sitting in the dirt under the cloud. The three of them, two horses and Denneyse, were looking at him.

"You ok?" she asked, hesitant to laugh.

"You know this is getting pretty embarrassing," he said. "I don't think guys are supposed to fall off into dirt piles in front of girls they are trying to impress."

"Well," she sat back in her saddle, "that was pretty darned impressive Joe." She was grinning now.

Joe stood and brushed off.

"Yup, pure embarrassin'. Only thing more impressive than my little stunt are all those spider webs hanging off your baseball cap." Denneyse reached up and pulled off her cap.

"Ugh," she said. "Disgusting."

"What was that orange thing anyway?" Joe asked.

"I don't think your horse likes the covers that SCE&G put on the valves for the buried gas lines," Denneyse said. "But," she smiled. We could work on that. Let's see, we could have, I know; how about Gas Valve Covers 101, how's that?" She was laughing. Then she shouted. "Beat you to the pond." Joe barely grabbed America's reins when she put her heals into Georgee Girl, and was off. He swung into the saddle and sped after her. They raced down, down over the hill. Denneyse was in the lead. Man, she was riding. Joe was admiring her cute backside on the pretty mare in front of him. He told America that; "If he was a clever horse he wouldn't let that mare get away." He was grinning and watching and riding, then there was the pond and that little mare stopped, just like a world class reining horse. By golly, like a flash, that pretty lady was in the pond, her baseball cap afloat.

"Hi there," Joe laughed, pulling to a stop at the water's edge. "This is not part of the lesson I had in mind," he shrugged, "but it's a start."

"I just wanted to wash off the spider webs," Denneyse smiled sweetly.

"Sure."

Georgee Girl walked to the edge of the water and stuck her nose in.

"May as well climb on her. I don't think the possibility of you getting wet if Georgee decides to take a swim will be a problem now," he laughed.

That was the summer of 1990, and they had begun really riding.

CHAPTER 11

Denneyse drove her Chevy Suburban to Greenville Friday evening to meet Joe at the Barn Yard dance. She was navigating the narrow streets of the older sections of Greenville, and had arrived early to walk awhile and enjoy the sights.

The old courthouse was on a tree-lined side street. The town clock was attached to the front of a thirty-foot tower beside the courthouse. Denneyse stopped in front of the clock tower and read the brass inscription. The clock had been installed during reconstruction after the War Between the States ended. Further down the sidewalk, heading north, was a low-slung building used as the town hall. It had a full-length over-hanging porch. The town hall building was adorned with a bright red tin roof. Joe told her the roof was the pride of the town residents and the latest town renovation project. He was laughing when he told her that the roof made front page news for weeks. Not a lot happened on a day-to-day basis in Greenville. That's when he told her about Lucy and the Jamboree Boys playing country hits every Friday and Saturday nights.

She was waiting for him inside, in the dark near the dance floor. The bar was enormously long with beautifully polished hard wood. She was watching the young couples' dance. It amused her that Lucy and the boys seemed to be pushing fifty, and she wondered how long they had been playing music for the Barnyard Dances. But it was easy to let their music move her, and soon she was tapping her foot and humming along.

Several young men at the bar were watching her, as she stood alone with her drink in her hand. Each had their separate thoughts. One thought they had in common was that she would not be standing alone for long.

Country music was Joe's favorite. The last time he had danced to Willie and Waylon was right before Nicole left him. He hadn't thought of Nicole in a long time, but he hadn't cared much about dancing until now, either. Denneyse was so much fun, often times he hadn't thought of her as a girl, only as a friend that he liked to be with. Not that she didn't look like a girl, but they were into enjoying the horses so much lately and working so hard, their relationship hadn't gotten into a boy-girl kind of thing. Joe smiled as he walked into the lobby. He really enjoyed being with D. They laughed a lot and he was relaxed with her. She didn't make him feel he had to be macho all the time. He felt like he could screw up, and it was no big deal.

Joe stepped up to the ticket counter. The chubby lady turned and smiled at him.

"Well, hey, stranger, I haven't seen you for so long," she giggled and patted his hand.

"Well, it's hard to put away old habits, isn't it, Mary?" Mary laughed. She was cute in a chunky blonde sort of way. She had hair that looked like it was on the verge of explosion. He figured her to be married with ten kids by now. He hadn't seen her since they had graduated from Camden High.

"What brings you up here?" he grinned.

"It's too hot in the valley, so I moved up here a couple of years ago," she chuckled. "It didn't do any good, still not married." She gave a frown and shrugged.

"Well, it's great seeing you, gotta go. I'm supposed to meet someone here." Joe motioned with his arm toward the lobby. "She's got long sandy colored hair and she's tall and..."

Mary's eyes went wide. "Yep, she's here; man, Joe, she's a looker, and that dress—oh, a figure to kill for in a dress like that. If she's not taken when you get in there I'll be surprised, and Joe she is sooo sweet." Joe looked at her surprised.

"Well, then maybe I'd better get on in there," he said.

"You all have a great time. Good seeing you." She reached out quickly and stamped his hand before he had time to jerk it away. He hated that ink stuff.

"It's ok, Joe—you can't see this stuff any more," Mary laughed. "Modern technology. We have a special light." She pointed to a blue light on the counter.

"Ok, good," Joe said and smiled. "See you later then, Mary."

"Only in my dreams," she muttered to herself.

He walked onto the crowded dance floor. His eyes tried to focus in the dim light. Where was she? He was looking around the floor. The band had already progressed to the belly bumping music, as he called it. It was slow and sexy. Jeez—where was she? His eyes came back to a tall woman standing alone a few steps from the bar, holding a glass. It was Denneyse. She was by herself, but he sure didn't know why. The bar light was playing off the dark blue of her short dress, which was low in front and above her knees. Actually, there weren't a lot of covered spaces in between. Her dress hugged her tiny waist, and the shortness of the skirt made her trim legs look as though they went on forever. He could see fine strands of her loosely curled hair floating in the glimmering light of the bandstand. Her hair was no longer pulled through her baseball cap, but fell soft over her shoulders, catching red and gold colors as the light flashed across the room. Good Lord, he thought, has she always looked like this and he was so ignorant that he never saw? She looked like an angel. He had a terrible urge to rush to her and hug her close. Fighting the urge, he stepped next to her and said, "You left your baseball cap at home?"

"Well," she smiled slyly, "I have an extra one out in the truck."

He stepped back and looked her over thoroughly. "Well on second thought," he smiled, "let's dance?" He offered her his hand.

"I thought you'd never ask," she said, and sat her glass down on the table next to her. She moved into his arms.

"You're much too beautiful to be standing all alone," he whispered into her ear.

"I knew it was time to take off my hat," she smiled against him. He didn't notice the music. He simply held her close.

CHAPTER 12

Crocus bloomed brightly in front of the cabin and along the pathway to the barn. Joe was happy that the cold winter was over. America had fared well, and as long as a miserable rain wasn't pouring down, Joe had left the horses outside in their paddock areas most of the winter. He believed in a horse living like a horse. His father practiced a similar philosophy. They believed this practice made for a happier, quieter animal.

Walking to his mailbox, Joe enjoyed spring's fresh greenery in the hardwood trees. The dogwood trees were also in full bloom; it looked like it had just snowed on them. Opening the box, he pulled out an orange flyer. "PLEASE JOIN US ON OUR ANNUAL SPRING FLING, APRIL 17, 1991, THE NIGHT OF THE FULL MOON—**MIDNIGHT RIDE** Sponsored by The Camden Hunt Club. This will be a novice endurance ride" the flyer read. "Those who wish to TRAIL ALONG AT YOUR OWN PACE MAY DO SO. For those who wish to participate in the endurance ride, we are asking for a donation of $15 per person, which will go toward prizes for the top five riders, and a meal at the End of Trail. Send your check and registration to Camden Hunt Club, General Delivery, Camden, S.C. 29680. A current coggins is required. A veterinarian will be on the grounds. See you there!"

Joe had been riding thirty or forty miles a week on America over the winter. He was unable to get down to Camden as often as he had wanted to. Though he knew that D was riding Georgee for Clyde at least four times a week, but he wasn't sure that the mare was in good enough condition to do an endurance ride. Heading for the telephone, Joe called D hoping that she could get the day off and go with him.

On April the 19th at 4 p.m., Joe and Denneyse pulled into the Camden Hunt Club parking area. Trailers and trucks were parked in rows, and people leading horses were moving back and forth across the parking lot. Horses were tied everywhere—from trailers, from trees, and tethered from ropes between trees. Most of the horses looked bored and were standing around swatting flies with their heads down.

The parking area was packed.

"Joe, look at all of those horses. Look over there," Denneyse said, pointing. "And look at that adorable pony. I have always wanted a pony like that if I ever have a little girl."

"Sounds like the wishes of a woman in love." Joe smiled as he maneuvered the truck and trailer into a parking spot under some trees away from the crowds. They parked and stepped out of the truck. The smell of roasting hot dogs was in the dusty air.

"Mmm, it smells wonderful here. I'm so excited." D said.

"LOOSE HORSE," some guy screamed. Then, suddenly a bay gelding raced through the aisle way dragging his lead line. The horse was running and bucking and having a good time in general. The apparent owner was the length of a football field behind and it didn't look promising.

"Hope he's in good condition, catching that horse could take awhile," Joe laughed. This is example one of what goes on at organized horse rides." He smiled. Joe opened the trailer latch on the exit door. He was still smiling when he said, "So—be sure to tie that mare good and I'll do the same. We don't need a paternity suit."

"Have you noticed the way that America looks at Georgee lately?" D had her eyebrows raised talking as she was brushing Georgee off.

"Oh, no you don't. Dad wants her to go to the Tevis in August if she does well this year. She isn't scheduled to be a stay at home mom just yet."

"Just wondered if you noticed."

"Dad won't give up on the idea of riding that race. Sure wish I could talk him out of it. I'll be worried the whole ride about him pushing himself to hard."

"If it's what he really wants, you can't tell him he shouldn't, you know?"

"I know. He's so hard-headed, if I did say anything about it he'd think it's because I was afraid that he might beat me."

"Is it?"

"Hey." Joe looked at her. "Well? No—I don't think so."

"Leave him be then; he is a grownup after all." D smiled, and changed the subject. "This place is full of those long-legged Anglo Arabs, have you noticed Joe?"

"Yeah, there's a bunch here," he agreed. He tied America on the other side of the trailer and wiped him down then sprayed fly spray on him.

"Wonder what the Bedouins would say if they saw these big old horses?"

"Not much," he said loudly. "They won the Crusades with the purebred Arabians; they were the size of a large pony. The small agile horses outmaneuvered the giants. To this day, we continue to outmaneuver them." He believed it too. "D," he said. "You should never let size intimidate you. A word of advice, your little mare may only be fifteen-hands high, but you can trust her to give all she's got. She will give you a great ride, D. I just know it. You just hang on."

"Ok," she said, "But look at that one moving out over there." Denneyse pointed. "He looks like he's marching to some alien tune. I never saw such long legs. Joe—this is scary." Her voice quivered with nervousness.

"Come on now." Joe pulled up the cinch on America's saddle. "We just agreed that tall isn't everything."

"Yeah, but I've never done this before. I mean, how do you know that Georgee won't be frightened with all the rowdiness going on. I think I'll just do the ride along thing."

"Oh no you don't" Joe attached the feedbag over America's head so that he could have his portion of oats. "Listen—just relax." An older gentleman walking by leading a white mare stopped and looked at America and Georgee.

"Those a really fine horses kids," he smiled. "Names Bill Riley. You all in the endurance competition or are you riding along?"

"We're doing endurance," Joe said. "It's our first time."

"Hey that's great, always like new young people coming on the rides. Me and Miss Lovely here," he scratched the mare's neck, "we're just riding along. I'm seventy," he beamed. "She's twenty-four this May."

"She is a beautiful mare," D exclaimed.

"Yes, I bet she was super as a youngster," Joe added.

The old man laughed. "That she was. We've covered a lot of trails. She's a Nabor granddaughter. Well, we must be getting back. I need to give some rations to her before too long. It was nice meeting you both. Me and Miss Lovely here wish you best of luck," he smiled.

"Nabor was one of the best, and one of America's finest imports." Joe was watching the pair walk away. "She's still going strong. That gives me a good feeling when I see a rider and a horse like that," he said.

"So don't be bugging your dad then," D grinned.

They walked toward the booth that was set up beside a vendor selling hot dogs. It was almost seven p.m. They would be riding in two hours, Denneyse was thinking. Her nerves were jumping just thinking about it. She was hoping she could do this. They had ridden the Hunt Club trails a lot. It was different at night, and this was serious riding instead of just playing around. Joe got their numbers and was attaching hers to the back of her long-sleeved cotton shirt.

"Just remember," he said suddenly hugging her waist from behind. "We sure as heck aren't here to win. We're just here to have fun. If this turns out to be fun, maybe you'll give me another date on a 100 miler?"

"Ok." She smiled brightly. "For fun." She hugged him back.

"But stick to me. Ok?"

"Ok," she said, looking at him suspiciously, wondering what that meant.

They were lined up haphazardly, milling around the starting line. The riders and horses that were going along for the ride were way behind the starting line.

"Never saw so many horses and riders here," D said. She was really nervous now. She had a death grip on her leather reins. Georgee was dancing around and wouldn't be still. "I don't know about all this Joe," she said nervously. Joe watched D. She was sitting tense in her saddle. He didn't want to worry about her, he wanted to concentrate on the ride, but he guessed he'd worry about her anyway.

"D, you need to ease up on Georgee and relax your seat in the saddle. She feels tension through your seat and legs."

"Well, she's a real smart horse then, cause I'm scared as hell," she replied a tremor in her voice.

"Listen, now if we get separated, which we probably will, just ride her and hold her back a little. You don't need to be up in the front in the first surge when all these crazy riders take off, ok?"

"Yes, ok," she shouted. "I'm going to walk her in a big loop right now and come back slowly, maybe she'll quiet some." Denneyse walked away from Joe and America. The other horses were stomping and snorting. People were yelling back and forth. Different riders and horses bumped Joe and America on both sides at the same time, trying to push ahead to get to the starting line. It was getting downright rude around here. Suddenly he couldn't even see Denneyse. Then the gun went off and the horses and riders surged forward in mass like a giant unstoppable machine.

Denneyse and the little mare were quickly shoved aside, and there was so much dust that if she hadn't seen the gray horses tail in front of her, she wouldn't have known which way to go. The little mare was feisty, much to her dismay. Suddenly, Denneyse didn't want to be where she was, and in fact, wondered if she wasn't quite insane for thinking that she had wanted to do this in the first place.

"Easy girl, easy," she said, as she firmly pulled back on the mare's reins. The mare did not want easy. Georgee wanted to go. Denneyse rode like that for about two miles; at least she thought it was two miles. She knew about where they were. She recognized the railroad track on the right-hand side and the gravel embankment which dropped off about five or six feet. Suddenly, out of the dark, two riders on two of the huge gray horses came up on her left and blasted her and Georgee off the embankment.

The little mare scrambled, trying desperately to gain a foothold on the loose gravel. The more that Georgee scrambled, the more mad Denneyse got with herself for getting her horse in this position. Had she been paying attention, instead of being a scared rabbit, her and her horse wouldn't be in danger right at this moment. She also could not believe the inconsiderate behavior of some of these people. At that point, she gave up trying to control

Georgee's balance and threw her arms around the mare's neck; the mare gained control of her equilibrium. D was holding onto the horse for dear life trying to stay forward as the mare climbed. Finally Georgee scrambled over the top of the embankment and they were off on the flat again. Denneyse was grabbing for the reins as they topped the bank trying to reestablish her control thing, when she realized that the mare was no longer nervous, and that they were flying over the ground. As she found her reins, she thought to herself, "Ok we can do this." She relaxed and began to ride.

Joe was in front somewhere with the first surge of riders. There was no way of telling what place, but there was still a dust trail in the moon light, so he knew there were riders up there. He hadn't seen Denneyse since they had started. He had to believe that she would be ok. He knew there were plenty of riders pulling up the rear if she had problem, and he felt sure someone would help her. He also thought that the mare had a lot more heart than Denneyse was giving her credit for, and if she would just sit the mare, he knew the horse would take care of the rest.

Joe recognized the area that they were in. The hill that they were coming to was the one that went down to the black water pond. It was he and Denneyse's favorite spot. America and Georgee loved this place too. America was cantering easily down the hill. Joe estimated that they had traveled about ten miles now and they had passed a lot of riders trotting their horses. Joe had pulled the stallion down a few paces passing others, but America clearly wanted to canter. So be it, he thought. In a few more miles there was a checkpoint with a vet. If they were going at it too strong, he figured the vet would pull him. In any case, he meant to let the feel of the horse determine their speed. This was a test. He cantered up behind a very large gelding whose backside was the size of a barn. The gelding was slow, and it slowed America's momentum, but it occurred to Joe that if it had been windy—this would be the animal to ride behind. They stayed in this position for another mile or two, and they moved to swing around the horse and rider. The gentleman aboard the gelding waved to Joe as they passed. The guy's face was smeared with dirt and had only two white spots where his eyes were, but his white teeth were shining in the moonlight. Joe was laughing and he patted America's shoulder. He wondered if his face looked the same, he figured it did.

Joe knew the slope down to the pond by heart. This was one of their favorite places, but this time he was riding into the pond from a different angle. The hill was steeper here, and he could barely see to the bottom. As they galloped closer, Joe realized that the cluster of riders and their willful mounts, which had refused to enter the pond, where causing a jam. It looked like total chaos, and he didn't want any part of it. The embankment above the riders and horses was ten feet higher than the pond. None of the riders were at the water. America was coming on fast, and the horse knew the pond was there and Joe knew America could smell it. He pulled on the reins to slow him, and not for the first time since the ride had begun, America stuck his nose out and galloped on.

Sliding and galloping down the bank, skidding on his hindquarters, America found room between the crowd and went off the bank into the water with a great leap. This was, after all, *his* swimming hole. Swimming strong, America gained the opposite bank. On his second step out of the water, he stopped and shook. Joe looked back and saw the group of riders standing still staring at him. Turning America, Joe went on down the trail.

Denneyse was not far behind and gaining ground. The mare was cantering easily now that D had relaxed in the saddle. Denneyse was letting the mare pick and choose her gaits. They had begun the ride unsure of themselves, but had quickly gained confidence, and the miles were clicking by. Denneyse felt the horse settle into her rhythm and they were both enjoying this ride. The other riders were spread out. They came up beside the gentleman riding the huge gray gelding cantering along all by himself.

"Hi," she yelled to him. "Would you happen to remember a dark-bay-stallion pass by with a young man riding him. He has a bright orange shirt on that says Clemson?"

"Sure do. He passed me about fifteen minutes ago," he yelled back to her. "He followed us for a while, then flew by. That's a right good looking mare." The guy winked at her.

"Thanks," she yelled to him saluting and laughing because it was an odd place to flirt. She swiped at her cheek, which had a fine coating of mud and sand on it. But she was tickled that they were moving up in the field. Denneyse reached to rub the mare's neck. Anyway, she thought, feeling suddenly superior, no one's bumping into us and pushing us into the bramble anymore. The pond was next.

Joe and America had dropped down into a marshy area. America was sucking through the mire and Joe had slowed him to a trot. The stallion took the muck easily. Joe could see through tall oaks growing in the marsh. He could tell that a creek was at the bottom and the clear area beyond. People were gathered on the other side and he figured it must be the vet check. The night had become chilly and steam was coming from the horse's nostrils; it was also rising from the horse's necks and bodies, making them look eerie in the moonlight.

Approaching the creek, Joe was surprised to see a flat wooden bridge without rails. The bridge was only three feet wide and about ten feet long, just long enough to cross the stream. There was a drop of two feet to the bridge, and the bank was slick and spooky. Ten horses refused to cross the bridge and there wasn't much space to give riders room to try the crossing. One big black horse was walking on his hind legs. It didn't look wise to join the foray. Joe hesitated, but America followed his nose, slid down the slope on his haunches, squatted, and sprang to the other side of the creek.

"Well, that takes care of that problem, doesn't it, boy," Joe laughed. They rode into the checkpoint at a canter. He figured he had a fifty-fifty chance of being pulled from the race. They had traveled fast, and he didn't know if he should have held the young stallion in some. Clyde saw Joe coming. He was waiting with Pepsi and carrots.

"Hey," Joe shouted, "how did you know we were down here?"

"I have my ways," Clyde laughed. "Doc told me Denneyse and you would be at this checkpoint, she gave me directions there and told me I could drive down to it, so here I am. How's he doing?"

"Man, dad, he's doing great. We'll have to go through the check here before I know for sure."

"Keep an eye out for Denneyse." Joe turned and looked up the trail he'd just come down.

"I thought she'd be with you."

"No, we got separated."

"Well, don't worry," Clyde shrugged, holding America's lead rope. "All of the reports on riders have been good. I know she's fine. I'm staying here until I see how their doing, so you get on with the business at hand. I need to see how my mare's doing, too," he grinned.

The vet and his assistant walked up to them.

"Gentlemen," the vet smiled. He bent over and started picking up America's feet one at a time. "How we doing here?" he asked.

"Well, ok, I think," Joe said.

"You been riding him hard?"

"I sort of let him choose. I wasn't pushing him into anything he didn't want to do. He wanted to canter most of the way. He seemed ok with it. Mostly, I've just been sitting on him."

"Well," the vet said, "let me listen here," and he put his stethoscope on America's chest and ribcage.

"Good, good." The vet walked around the stallion. "Very nice horse, Mr. Joe Richards, number 233." He looked at Joe's number on America's butt and checked his list to find Joe's name. "Ah yes, very nice horse, heart checks rested rate. You can be on your way sir, in ten minutes," he checked his watch. "Ten more minutes," he warned, shaking his finger at Joe.

"Yes sir," Joe grinned. "Good luck son." He waved at Joe and walked to the next horse.

"See there, that horse is just like his sire," Clyde clapped Joe on the back.

"Pretty good, huh?" Joe said.

"Pretty good. There's eighty-seven horses here, son. I think you're up there pretty close."

"Well, we're not really racing." Joe insisted.

"Sure," Clyde sniffed. "Well, let me get this bucket and stuff out of the way so you—ah—can't race." Clyde smiled and started moving the bucket and towel and sponges. He looked up just in time to see Denneyse and Georgee approaching. "Hey, there's my girls," Clyde yelled. Denneyse and Georgee trotted right up to them. Georgee stopped as D was swinging out of the saddle.

"Hey you," Joe laughed. He was already mounted and ready to ride. "I'm on my way out, but it sure is good to see you. Doing ok?"

"Doing great now," D grinned. Boy do I have stuff to tell you."

"Good ride D," Joe wished her, and waved as they turned and trotted away.

"Good ride, Joe," she yelled. "Come on Clyde, where's that vet? Let's get her checked—I want to beat them bad," she grinned.

"That's my girl," Clyde grabbed Georgee's lead and started mixing his special formula trail mix for the mare. Joe was passing a few riders who were laughing and chatting among themselves. The big gray horses were in single file and trotting along at a ground-eating pace. America was cantering slow and easy behind them, but he felt the stallion want to change gears and pass. They were going along the 500 KV power line road, and it was open and desolate-looking landscape in the moonlight. Joe knew that they would travel the power line road another mile or so, and he asked America to come back to an extended trot. He didn't want to chance exhaustion; after all, he wasn't really racing, was he?

He looked behind him and there was another rider passing a gray horse and coming on at a good clip. He thought it was Denneyse, but how could that be? Another mile out and he turned again.

"Hey you, wait for us," she yelled. It was Denneyse.

"You thought you could ditch us huh?" She rode up beside Joe and America.

"Well, I see you're getting the hang of it?" Joe smiled and they trotted along. "Your pony tail is really different." It hung limp and glued together behind her hat.

"It was the pond that did it, I guess," she laughed. "We jumped in, and by golly she jumped so far I almost came off. I had no idea she could jump like that. Guess she wanted to be away from the crowd in a hurry. Believe me, no one got in our way crossing that pond. She scrambled, coming out the other side, and the horse in front of us was throwing sand and mud everywhere. Anyway, voilá, a new do." She tilted her head at him, smiling. Joe was watching her animation through her story.

"You're a real cow girl, you know that?" he said.
They moved up beside two riders that were buddying up. One horse was black, the other was white. The white horse

was heaving and having a rough go of it. America eyed the horse and sidestepped around them.

"Wonder how far back from the front we are?" Denneyse asked.

"Don't know," Joe said

"Well, we've got Devils ridge and the flat and we're home, no matter," Joe said.

"Yep—no matter. But we're not racing anyway, so it really doesn't matter." Denneyse said.

"That's right, I know we're not." Joe grinned. He glanced at his watch. "It's midnight," he shouted to her. Somehow, that seemed significant. They looked at each other. "Does that mean we're racing?" Joe yelled. They were both cantering side by side now.

"Dern right we're racing," she yelled, and looked straight ahead and forgot all about what they had agreed to do. Suddenly they were flying. The wiry Arab horses jumped forward. They were good at the scramble and best climbing a hill. They were nimble little horses with round fat feet that laughed at rock, gravel, and sand. They were making tracks, making time, and beating the big guys. They were bred for sure-footedness, and the speed of light. The stallion named America and the mare called Georgee Girl were driving hard for the finish. Joe could feel the power under him as the horse surged up Devils Ridge. America gobbled up the ground as if he were starved for it. The leather of the saddle creaked with the pressures of the horse's shoulders and back moving beneath it. America, with nostrils extended full, stretching out his long graceful neck, bounded up and over the ridge. They hit the flat ground below wide open. Joe looked back.

Georgee Girl was only a half a length behind him, her legs flashing in the moonlight. He felt America downshift and hit a stride that he had never before felt. It was pure power. Right at that moment it came to him that somehow fate had chosen only him to be here at this moment on this horse to experience this feeling of power. It was indescribable. The wind screamed past his ears, his eyes watered. He knew that this horse was destined to go to the Tevis cup. He knew it more than he knew anything. Lights ahead were flashing behind trees. He could see them, and he knew they were almost to the finish line.

Denneyse and Georgee Girl were close behind. Georgee's wide nostrils blew white in the moonlight. She was a devil horse. Her ears were flat on her head, and she was stretched full out. The mare was intent on the win. Joe could feel it in her, though he wasn't on her. There were two riders pulling up from behind. Joe lay down over America's neck and started singing, of all things, at the top of his lungs. He sang and he sang over the creaking of the leather, over great breaths of air. The horse ran on, pushing his body to the limit. Hooves were pounding, wind was screaming by. Still Joe sang Willy's song, "You ain't a gonna catch me now, you ain't a gonna catch me now— Midnight Rider!!" Joe Richards and Denneyse Danner raced under the finish line one and two.

"My bottom is a pancake!" Denneyse screamed as she pulled back on Georgee for all she was worth. She was laughing, Joe was laughing. He felt relief and tremendous elation. People were suddenly everywhere hugging up around the steaming horses and the two young people who had dismounted from them. Clyde appeared and reached for Joe's reins. He was grinning from ear to ear.

"What kept ya boy?"

"We wanted to be sure everyone had time to get here and get our breakfast ready. We're starved." Dr. Cindi was behind Clyde, with Susan. Cindi was laughing.

"My-my, it's amazing what nature and science can create." She smiled. Joe hugged America's neck. Dr. Cindi was listening to the horse's heart rate. "He is simply unreal," she spoke quietly. "The gray flannel crowd is going to be miffed, you know? By the way, I would like to know what you're charging this year for, stud fees?"

"Really?" Joe asked.

"Most definitely," Susan butted in.

"You let us know what his fee schedule is, Joe. I, for one, don't want to wait until I can't afford him." Susan teased.

Denneyse threw her mud-encrusted cap into the air and shouted. Joe caught her around the waist and pulled her close. He whispered in her ear, "Marry me?" She pulled back and looked into his eyes.

"I'll marry you, but you have to promise to stick to horses, Joe."

"Stick to horses?"

"Yes, you're really a lousy singer," she grinned.

CHAPTER 13

"I ain't wearen no dern pantyhose, I don't care how many blisters I get. Golly Susan - it's the principal of the thing, you know?" Clyde complained. Susan was standing in front of Clyde holding a pair of brown panty hose.

"You're the most aggravaten' man I've ever met in my entire life, Clyde Richards. Here you are about to embark on one of the most important thrills of your life and your too pig-headed to listen to recommendations from riders that have ridden the Tevis ride for years."

"Listen, if they won this ride by riding a jackass, I wouldn't go out an' buy a jackass, would I? No, I would not. An' if they won this ride by wearen' pantyhose, I would not go out and get me some pantyhose either," Clyde yelled.

"You're the jackass, Clyde Richards," Susan said totally exasperated with him.

"You are so pretty when you're mad," Clyde grinned.

"You did not listen to a thing I said, Clyde. You should always be open-minded enough to profit from others' progress."

"Well I've always done things my way and I may not win, but I'll have my dignity, now won't I?"

"Ok, ok. I give up." She threw the pantyhose on the armrest of his couch. "You are just a hard-headed old man," she said. "Do what pleases you, you usually do. I'm going home now." She kissed him quickly on his cheek, even though Clyde knew she was not happy with him. "See you at dinner. I am fixing a leg of lamb today. If you feel the need of good company, it'll be ready at 7."

"Good," he said. "You make the best lamb in the country."

"Don't try to butter me up, Clyde Richards." She cut her eyes sharply at him. He held his hands palm up.

"Alright, truce?"

"For now," she conceded, and was out the front door. He watched her drive off, dust flying. Well, he thought, walking and talking to himself all the way to the barn to saddle Georgee. She was probably right, but he wouldn't tell her that. It was just a sissified thing to do is all, pantyhose of all things.

Saturday morning Joe called the ranch. Susan picked up the telephone.

"Morning Joe," Susan sounded sleepy. Joe smiled into the telephone. His dad's life at sixty-two was amazing to him. One of the town's most beautiful women was camped out at his father's ranch.

"Sorry if I woke you." Joe said.

"That's ok. I should have been up an hour ago," Susan said.

"Is dad there?"

"Nope, he's out on his six mile walk."

"Are you kidding?"

"No, it's true," Susan smiled.

"Isn't it raining down there? It is here."

"Sure is."

"Well I guess he's serious then. He really is going to do the Tevis Ride?"

"I am sure he is," Susan said. "I think his goal is to teach a thing or two to the younger generation. Rain or shine, he is out there whipping himself into shape, or something."

"Should I call around noon, do you think?"

"He comes in to eat his rabbit food then. So that will probably be good."

"No meat and potatoes any more, huh?"

"Not very often. He has lost twenty pounds, Joe. I believe he weighs about one eighty now. Believe it or not, he's trying to get to one sixty-five."

"But that's nothing but skin and bone," Joe protested.

"I told him that, but he hasn't taken a lot of my advice lately. He is totally focused on this Tevis ride."

"Well, I'll be." Joe said.

"When he comes back from his walk here in a little while, he goes down and gets Georgee and exercises her. There is no grass growing under that old man's feet." She laughed.

"I can see that. That ride will be harder than a marathon. He's probably doing the right thing. I'll try him later. But if I miss him, will you tell him or leave a note where he can see it that I'll be down tomorrow morning? I'm bringing America, and D would like to ride Georgee. We're going to go over to the hunt club."

"How's the long distance romance going?" she asked.

"You know—I've got my job and she has to finish her apprenticeship. I don't know what we're going to do just yet. We'd like to get married in the fall, but Dr. Cindi has offered her a really good position to stay there. Cindi wants to work all the AI cases and she wants D to cover all the routine calls, including some of the emergency calls. We love Cindi, no one more than Denneyse, so we have a dilemma."

"Joe, I have found that anything that is worth a darn usually has at least some dilemma to it. It'll work out somehow, you'll see. Meantime, I'll leave your dad a note, because I'm going to be on my way in just a minute. You take care," she said.

Joe stood looking at the receiver. Six miles? His father was amazing. He even felt that competitive adrenaline spring up inside himself. He thought that a foolish feeling to be having. After all, he was in his twenties and his dad in his sixties. My gosh, his father was competing against him. That fact alone made the feeling feel even more foolish. Thinking about it being foolish, however, did not make the adrenaline buzz leave.

Sunday morning found Joe unloading America from the horse trailer; the stallion was prancing and dancing. Georgee called to them from her stall, which only got him more excited.

"This is not the time buddy, Joe told his horse. He put America into the stall furthest from Georgee. He walked to the house humming a tune and thinking of Denneyse. She would be here any time now. His dad stepped out the back door of the house.

"Man, look at you, dad," Joe whistled. "Slim and trim." Clyde patted his flat belly.

"Fighten' weight." He grinned. "Here, hit me hard as you can right here," Clyde dared Joe.

"I can't do that," Joe said. "What if I killed my only dad?"

"Ahh, Clyde smiled, "no way. You have competition, son," Clyde raised his eyebrows and narrowed his eyes at Joe.

"I already knew that." Joe grinned and there was that feeling rising within. For the life of him, he couldn't figure why he got that surge when he was certain that his father would be pushing him, trying to beat him.

"Listen Dad, you sure it's ok if D takes Georgee to the club today?"

"Sure, that's not a problem. Susan said you all were meeting up here this morning. Go ahead, she's ready. It'll be good for her. Keep in mind she's in season. I don't want that rake of yours harrassen' my filly," Clyde joked.

"He's good," Joe laughed.

"Well, I know he's good, but he ain't dead, ya know." I got me a tape on the Tevis ride the other day in the mail. I want you to watch it before you go home tonight."

The phone rang in the house. "I'll get it," Clyde said. He turned and bounded into the house.

"My, my, we are spry," said Joe. Clyde came back.

"Go on in there, it's D."

"Hi," Joe said. "Oh really? Me too. No, that's ok, I understand. Sure, we'll go get a steak tonight at the Road House. Love you, ok, bye."

"Sounds like you got stood up."

"They have a mare they have to do an emergency surgery on. Then she has to keep her eye on the mare. Cindi got another call and has to get on the road. Oh well."

"Well hey, just so it isn't a wasted trip, how 'bout I go with you." Clyde grinned.

"Sure, great. She is your horse after all," Joe said. "Now it can get sort of hairy out there, you know dad."

"No problem." Clyde smiled. "I've been riding since you were a twinkle in your mothers' eye." (Joe had been saying the words right along with him on the last four words).

"I know, I know," he smiled. "Let's load up then."
Joe's gut feeling was not to go, but since he'd already been having strange sensations about competing with Clyde in the endurance race, he wasn't going to say anything about it. He wondered if he was really worried about Clyde or worried that Clyde just might win. He wasn't sure which it was. He loaded the horses and he kept his mouth shut.

They started the ride at an extended trot, easily crossing over the railroad bed and all the gravel. When they came to the hill that was Joe's favorite trail, he put America into a rolling canter. Georgee, with Clyde aboard, stayed right on America's heels. The trail rose and narrowed a bit and became only wide enough for a horse to pass. Run off water had gouged the trail deeper. Georgee was still right behind. America was cantering contently with the mare following nicely.

Both horses pulled at the bit and they were in an easy relaxed gate. Joe glanced back; his dad was grinning. Joe rode past several trail markers. Then the Fire Tower Road sign appeared, and he veered to the left. Now they were moving smartly down the big power line trail in a hand gallop, hooves pounding the wide road with its sandy loam. The double creek crossing appeared and they approached in a gallop and plunged through the first of the shallow creeks. Joe was still in front when Clyde surged forward passing them. For a second, Clyde and the mare were beside him and America, and then they were ahead. They splashed into the second creek full out when the little mare stumbled and almost went to her knees. Clyde stayed in the saddle, but barely. Joe was already pulling America back. They came to a halt on the other side of the second stream. Clyde jumped off the mare and lifted her left front foreleg. He reached into the back pocket of his jeans and drew out his hoof pick. There was a stone lodged between the wall of the hoof and the metal of her shoe, and he popped it out.

"Well, ain't that dandy?" he said and remounted. Clyde queued the mare forward and she hopped, then lifted the weight off of her left fore. "Oh my word," he said sliding off of her again. "How far have we come?"

"About two miles, more or less," Joe answered. "Here." He unsnapped America's lead rope from the stallions neck. "Hook this on her halter and climb up behind me. We better take her out to the clinic and have D get an x ray of that foot." The ride back to the trailer was very quiet. A lame horse would not be going to the Tevis. Joe wondered if his gut reaction to coming out this morning had anything to do with this.

"I had a bad feeling about coming this morning after Dennyese cancelled," Joe told Clyde.

"Really?"

"Yes, but I thought if I said anything about it you might think that I just didn't want to ride with you."

"Now why would I think that?"

"You know. I really want to win. You really want to win too."

"Not at any cost," Clyde said. I would have listened to you."

"I didn't say anything because I thought you might think that I didn't want to ride with you because I wouldn't want you to win."

"You win, I win, doesn't matter. Just so a Richards wins. That's what I think," Clyde laughed. "Two chances are better than one."

An hour later, Denneyse put the x-ray film up on her screen. "Well, it's a pretty bad stone bruise. Good news is it isn't serious." She smiled. Just then Cindi came into the office.

She walked over, frowning at the film shining in the light.

"She's right, but the bad news is, it will mean three to four weeks in a stall."

"No," Clyde said. He looked about to cry.

"But the Tevis Cup."

"She won't make it this year, Clyde. She will be out of condition by the time she's healed, and possibly it could take her another week or two of rest. She needs to be confined to heal. I'm really sorry." Cindi reached out and patted his shoulder.

"Well." Clyde removed his hat and wiped his brow. "Guess we best get them on home, 'eh, doc?"

"Yes." Cindi turned and looked at him.

"Won't hurt to breed her will it?"

"Clyde, I don't think that part of her is wounded," she smiled.

"Right, right. Thanks doc."

When they got home, Clyde said, "You go on and let America breed that mare son. She's in season now and it's a good time of year anyways."

"Dad I'm sorry about the cup and all," Joe said.

"It's nothing that can be helped. You know there is a reason things happen in life. No use to question them. I made one trip all the way to California, maybe that was what I was supposed to do. America may turn out to be the best thing I've done my whole life. We'll make the best of it. That's what the Richards family does. However, I'm going in to get me a beer. Maybe that'll cheer me some." Clyde walked on to the house.

"Hey dad," Joe yelled at him.

"Yeah?" Clyde turned.

"Best thing you've done is be my dad."

"Well, thank you, son." Clyde smiled.

CHAPTER 14

During the Crimean War (1851-1854), one Arab horse raced ninety-three miles without harm, but its rider died from exhaustion.

The Sierra National Forest is 1.3 million acres in central California on the western slope of the Sierra Nevada mountain range south of the Merced River and north of the Kings River. The terrain ranges from gently rolling, oak-covered foothills along the edge of the great San Joaquin valley, to the majestic snow-capped peaks of the Sierra Nevada crest.

Joe was reading from a travel brochure that he received before they left home.

"Listen to this. This is really interesting, dad. During the gold rush years of the early 1800s, there was a great deal of gold prospecting and mining activity. Gold panning and dredging are still popular. So if you fall in the river, maybe you'll come up with a few nuggets?"

"Least ways it'll make our trip worth while," Clyde said.

"Listen, dad. Much of the area's water supply flows from the National Forest Lands. There are over 480 lakes and 1,800 miles of streams and rivers."

"Hope you threw in the trolling motor Joe."

"Hey, listen to this. The National Forestry Lands are still wild and remote. It is home to over three hundred species of wildlife including coyote, bobcats, beavers, foxes, porcupines, deer, and black bear."

"Reckon they have rednecks up here?" Clyde asked.

They topped the ridge of the Sierra Nevada range on highway 80 heading west into Truckee. They drove until they saw the turn for highway 267 and followed the directions through town. When they found the forestry road #6 they turned right toward Robie Park.

"Can you imagine this country a hundred and fifty years ago?" Joe asked. He was excited. "A body can't see into all of those cracks and crevasses up there in those mountains, I bet it's a piece of work in there."

"Lot of it doesn't look fit for a good goat, son. These are young mountains, still moving around too. These mountains aren't like our Blue Ridge Mountains, worn nice and smooth, lots of trees and grass. Myself, I lean toward a more accommodating land." Clyde nodded. "But I suppose it's the wildness that's exciting. You're right son, you know that's exactly why all those crazy guys came here too, but I'll be a might happier when you cross that finish line and you're safe." That was the end of that. Joe had not said a word to Clyde about his decision that Clyde was the one that would ride America.

"Look there," Clyde pointed, "here we are." He pulled off the highway into the marked parking area of Robie Park. Huge banners were popping in the breeze.

WELCOME TO THE 54TH ANNUAL GREAT WESTERN STATES TEVIS ENDURANCE RIDE - please follow signs and proceed to designated parking area and check-in booth.

They unloaded America and got him settled in a stall next to two geldings. Then Joe went to get his paper work in order. He had his vet records in hand. Joe left Clyde talking to a neighbor competitor, a lady of sixty-eight years young. Clyde was doubled over laughing as the woman told him, "If I don't get a buckle for a finish this year, I'm going to take one off of someone's body before I leave this place." From the looks of the feisty old woman, Joe figured she just might be able to do that.

Joe was standing in line. There was a wood-framed, glass-covered park sign that he was reading about the Tevis Cup.

The Tevis Cup was named for Lloyd Tevis (1824-1899) by his grandson Will Tevis, a prominent San Francisco businessman and early benefactor of the Ride. The trophy is awarded to the first rider to complete the 100-mile Ride whose mount is "fit to continue." It was first awarded in 1959 to Nick Mansfield, riding Buffalo Bill, an eleven-year-old Thoroughbred Cross gelding. The Trail goes from the Lake Tahoe Area to Auburn. It is said that the Ride has 19,000 feet of "up" and 22,000 feet of "down".

"Next," a man standing behind the counter said, trying to get Joe's attention. Joe presented the inoculation certificates and vets examine records on America.

"I need to make a change of rider," Joe smiled at the man.

"First time?"

"Yes, but I want my father to ride my horse."

"Oh? It's usually the other way around." The guy grinned. "The old folks get a look at the terrain and they start signing the horses over to the young folks. Well—just need his name. I'll fix up your change and assign the number to him. He'll be riding a stud horse?"

"Yes sir."

"Ok, we'll mark the horse's butt this evening with paint. Says stud," he grinned, "Just to let everyone know to use a bit of caution. It gets narrow on the trail."

"That's what I've heard," Joe remarked.

"Your father in shape for this?"

"Yes sir. He's been walking six miles a day and riding quite a bit. He was bringing a mare, but she came up lame. He really wanted to do this ride," Joe explained.

"So you're giving him your horse?"

"Yes, sir."

"You're all right," the man said and reached across the counter and shook Joe's hand. "Wish your father luck for me, will you."

"Yes, sir." Joe smiled.

Clyde met him when he returned to the truck and trailer. He was holding a bundle with a blanket thrown over it.

"What is that?" Joe stared at the bundle.

"Something I want to give to you for this ride," he grinned. Clyde drew the blanket away. Joe looked at it. Clyde looked from the saddle he had unveiled to Joe. "What? It's a Calvary saddle," he explained. "This baby is like new. I tried it on him and rode him with it on one day when you were off on an errand. It's perfect."

"There's a crack down the middle," Joe frowned.

"That is how they are made," Clyde said getting exasperated.

"Listen dad, I've got to go turn in America's AERC records so they know he'd completed the required mileage to enter."

"Ok, Ok, you go on then," Clyde waved him on. He placed the saddle on a bale of hay and brushed it lightly with his hand. "It's a family thing," he said to himself. "It'll bring him luck."

In about fifteen minutes, Joe returned. He handed Clyde the entry form copy and a bright orange vest with the number 254. Clyde looked down at the entry form.

"This thing has my name on it," he said and looked up at Joe. "Why?"

"You've been dreaming of this ride forever." Clyde started to protest. "No," Joe held up his hand.

"America is your horse, son,"

"I know, but I've got next year, and besides, I wouldn't have him without you. He has the blood that you bred for all those years. Just think, dad. The stallion you're riding is carrying the bloodline of Bint Nefsoud and Hoshaba thundering through these canyons. I can see it dad. I can feel what it's going to be, out there in those places. Tomorrow will be your day, yours and America's. I have next year." Joe shoved the vest back into Clyde's hand. "Besides, I think you should ride in that saddle." He smiled. Clyde's brain shifted from the mystical rendition that Joe had just recited to the comment about the saddle.

"You wouldn't be doin' all this just so you wouldn't have to sit in my saddle?"

"No," Joe laughed. Clyde sat down on the wooden bench behind him. His legs felt woozy. He couldn't think of anything intelligent to say so he just said, "Holy cow, Joe."

"Yeah," Joe agreed. "Better get yourself over there and weigh in and do the drug screening."

"Drug screening on me?"

"Of course not, on America. He needs his vet exam and drug screening. Then we're going to change out his shoes to some of those lightweight things they have. You ride at 5:15 a.m. We have to get our ducks in a row, dad. Welcome to the TEVIS."

At 4:30 A.M. pots and pans were clattering. Handlers were leading horses behind them, passing back and forth in the dark. Some of the handlers had on funny helmets with lights on them.

"Here's coffee, dad." Joe handed Clyde a cup that was steaming in the cool morning air. Clyde gulped it and sat the cup on the truck hood.

"Here, put these under your riding pants." Joe was holding up a pair of panty hose in his right hand.

"You too. I can't believe this. First Susan, now you."

"Listen dad, I was going to wear these. Trust me, it's the smart thing to do."

"It's a conspiracy, that's what." Clyde grabbed the pantyhose and undid his pants, then slid them off.

"You wear these over them," Joe handed Clyde a pair of English riding pants.

Clyde looked up to the sky saying a prayer. "Please Lord, just ignore this newfangled mess and don't judge me by what I'll be a wearen' today."

"What in the world will everyone think," Clyde mumbled after his prayer.

"Everyone's wearing the same thing, dad." Joe rolled his eyes. "Here, eat this." Joe handed Clyde a biscuit with sausage and egg on it. "Now you have the insulated Gore-Tex jacket," he said going down his list.

"FIFTEEN MINUTES UNTIL RIDE TIME," the announcer called. Clyde's heart gave an involuntary lurch. What if he had a heart attack or something equally embarrassing, he thought to himself. Well, the heart attack would have to wait until later, he vowed. Please God, let it wait, he asked silently. He saw his lady friend, Rose Gillard, jog by, leading her horse. He vowed to ride behind her awhile. After all, she'd done this ride nine times. She probably knew the right things to do, especially while it was dark.

"Hey Rose," Clyde yelled.

"Hi Clyde. Ready?" she yelled.

"Sure am. Can we buddy up for awhile, Rose?"

"No problem. Come on now. I'm going to start right over here," she pointed.

"That's a good idea, dad." Joe smiled. He suddenly grabbed his dad in a bear hug.

"If there's someone I can get a ride up to with at a mid-point check, say, Michigan Bluff or Forest Hill, I'll be there." I'm going to call D and Susan as soon as I know you're off safe. Love you, dad."

"I love you too, Joe. I'll do my best."

"I know you will."

"TEN MINUTES," the announcer said. "RIDERS BRING YOUR HORSES FORWARD—LAST CALL."

The air was dusty even with the fog of early morning. It was the longest ten minutes that Clyde had ever lived. His mouth was dry. His hands were wet. He was hoping that his bowels didn't cut loose, he was so worked up. He mounted America. At least the Calvary saddle felt good on his butt. Riders on snorting horses were bumping against him. Several times he lost sight of Rose in the poor light. Luckily, she was riding one of those big gray animals. Between the white of the woman's hair and the white of the horse, they stood out. "10-9-8-7-6-5-4-3-2-1- GOOD LUCK RIDERS!" the announcer screamed.

Hundreds of horses carrying their riders plunged into total blackness. Horses rammed horses. One horse went down, another on top of it. Clyde's throat closed. Thoughts of doom raced through his brain as he fought to steer around one pile-up after another. This was scaring the hell out of him. Somehow he got through and around them without mishap, although he couldn't tell which direction he was going or what was ahead of him. He saw Rose on the big gray gelding posting primly up ahead and aimed America for her gelding's posterior. All he knew was that he was somewhere at the start of the Great Western States trail. How in the world the pioneers ever made it, he'd never know. He asked America for an extended trot and he planned to stay in it until he could see. Before he knew it, they were through Squaw Valley and on their way to Emigrant Pass.

Emigrant Pass would be the highest spot in the race at 8,700 feet. America felt strong beneath him. He wiggled his fingers, loosening his death grip on the reins. He began to sit the horse's rhythm and relax. Rose was two horses ahead. Two hundred and fifty horses had started, bunched together. Ten miles out, they were already stringing out. Hooves were striking stone and shale on the trail and he could see sparks flying from the strikes. He moved America around a horse and came up beside Rose.

"Hey you," she laughed. "You made it."

"So far," Clyde said.

"Never met anyone from South Carolina. Are there many Arabs out there?"

"Nope," Clyde said. "They like the warm bloods in our state."

"Yes, well, they do have their place, don't they?" She grinned.

"Suppose so, sure don't see them here, do we?"

"Well, this certainly isn't their place," she laughed.

"What comes next?" he asked her.

"We are working our way to 8,700 feet. It will freeze you to death. But it will be daylight at Emigrant Pass. It will be our fist vet check. We'll be twenty miles out."

"Well, I, for one, am thankful it will be light soon. This is scarier than riding a roller coaster at midnight," he said. She laughed at him.

"You ain't seen nothing yet, Hon," she yelled.

The forestry road turned into a footpath. They rode their extended trot during the entire climb into Emigrant Pass. It was spitting snow, of all things, in the middle of July. Clyde pulled his hat tight and zipped his jacket. Thank heaven for this newfangled material on his jacket. The path was strewn with rock and the dirt had long since turned to powder. The horses up ahead made clouds of dust, and coming down the other side turned out to be worse than going up. If it did snow, at least it would wet the ground.

In several spots, America was on his hindquarters sliding down the trail.

"Excuse us please," Clyde called to the riders who were walking down the bank.

They pulled to the right hand side and he moved on. It was a good fifteen miles of nothing but switchbacks and rocks. His spirits picked up a mite when the land leveled off. They came through a narrow gorge at a rolling canter but the canyon grew closer and closer and Clyde pulled America back to his trot. Clyde looked up—nothing but sky and what looked to be buzzards up there. Now it was really steep. Clyde wondered if this was the beginning of the Cougar Rock climb. They caught up with another rider. It was a young woman on a bay gelding moving along ahead of them.

"Hi," Clyde yelled. "Is this Cougar Rock?"

"Yes sir," the young woman answered. "Tough climb ahead, be careful. If your horse starts having trouble you can get off him and get behind him. Pump his tail like a water pump, then he'll get on up there," she advised.

Now why in the world would I want to do that to my horse? Clyde shook his head. How humiliating. Why would anyone suggest such a strange action was beyond him? America was scrambling and Clyde was standing up in his stirrups over the horse's neck. America slid on the shale and rock. Much to Clyde's horror the horse began bounding from boulder to boulder. He even seemed to hesitate to measure each leap. Clyde looked to his left and looked to his right, which wasn't comforting at all. There was at least a two hundred foot drop on each side. Clyde was holding his breath between each leap. Up, up they went. Clyde wound his fingers into America's thick mane and hung on for dear life. They topped the crest and some joker with a huge black-eyed camera, perched on a boulder like a toad, was sitting there. He snapped Clyde and America's picture before Clyde could yell an oath at him. Clyde bit his tongue, holding back the verbal thrashing he was about to give the camera buff. He had been worrying over falling two hundred feet and had run into the guy just willing to make it happen. Clyde wondered what he earned by perching on a boulder at 6,000 feet.

Cougar Rock climb took its toll on another thirty-four horses and one rider who was injured when his horse slid and rolled over him. The injuries were enough to pull the rider from the race. At the first vet check, they were down to two hundred and four riders. Clyde saw a gray mare standing with her feet splayed, foam mixed with blood coming from her nose. It was not a pretty sight. The horse's rider and vet were beside the mare.

America and Clyde rested, and the vet gave them his blessing. America had his fill of water, and ate oats with wet alfalfa cubes. Clyde had given America his share of electrolyte paste to check against dehydration, hosing him down and rubbing him thoroughly. Clyde believed in doing as much as possible for his horse. He thought that they were making excellent time. The timekeeper confirmed that they were, and said he thought there were only a couple of dozen riders ahead of them. Actually, he was surprised by their luck. He felt good too, for an old man. He attributed his well being to his horse's smooth action. It surely wouldn't do to ride a rough mount on this ride. They cantered out to find Robinson Flat.

They rode on to a forestry road and stayed in a canter. There were cedar trees growing throughout the area. The hardwood trees were gone. Up ahead it looked like they would get back into the forest. Clyde was looking forward to the ride in the forest. Robinson Flat was higher in elevation and so far, very nice for a canter. Clyde left no less than fifteen riders in his dust out on Robinson Flat. He hoped America would check out Ok at the next vet stop. They had really been pushing it.

He galloped through the forest and dropped down into a lovely grassy meadow. He rode past a granite stone with an inscription on it that said "Crossroads of the Sierra."

The afternoon sun was bright, the air crystal clear. Robinson Flat cheered him a mite. The mountains were formidable as they drew closer. He realized that Joe riding the stallion in the Blue Ridge Mountain foothills at the higher elevation had helped the stallion's stamina.

He slowed the stallion to a trot and then a walk as they came to the checkpoint. Clyde dismounted. He turned and looked back down the trail, he didn't see his friend Rose. In fact, he hadn't seen her in quite awhile. He had passed her about four hours ago, as soon as the gray of morning light had brightened the trail. He hoped she was doing well. If not, he pitied the poor fool whose belt buckle would surely be missing by morning.

It would be that thirty-two riders were disqualified at Robinson Flat. Apparently they had done what Clyde had done and galloped along in the forest enjoying the sights, but their horses weren't fit and did not pass the vet check. "Can you believe that?" a guy on a big black mare said to him as they left the Robinson Flat. "The vet was pulling horses left and right. I wonder how many were disqualified back there? We have only traveled about forty miles."

"I figured we lost at least that many just getting out of camp this morning," Clyde laughed. "I'm sure that was my imagination, being dark and all."

"That was a sight, wasn't it," the guy agreed. They rode side by side for the next ten miles or so. The guy was Jeff Leggitt from Georgia, another Johnny Reb. He had on panty hose too.

Clyde cut his eyes to Jeff; "You wear those panty hose too?" Clyde asked him.

"Huh? Oh yeah, everyone wears those things, keeps you from getting blisters on your whatever," he laughed. Clyde was beginning to feel like the panty hose thing had been a pretty decent idea. He thought he'd never make fun of those sissy-looking English riders again.

They were covered in trail dust. Even the horses had a fine layer on them. He could only imagine what his face looked like. Jeff looked like a raccoon.

He and Jeff were still buddied up as they rode into Last Chance. There was evidence of prospecting in the sides of the rocky hills in the remote area. They trotted out over a ridge where they could see the river down below the trail. This was a lonely place with nothing but the wind now. He wondered how many had been here in the 1800s trying to find their fortune.

"Lonely place," he said to Jeff.

"Wouldn't want to stay here unless I had a lot of food and a good woman and in that order," the young man said laughing.

The land seemed to go forever up in these hills and they were steadily dropping in elevation. Trotting along, they passed several riders who looked much the same as they did, dusty and tired.

"The other horses are slowing," Clyde remarked.

"I'm having trouble with my mare too. I have to keep after her. She wants to eat everything along the trail. Seems an excuse to stop to me," he said.

Clyde moved in front as they entered a narrow winding trail. They were moving down quickly into a green area. There was probably a stream close.

"You reckon we're coming to the Swinging Bridge?" Clyde yelled over his shoulder.

"Could be," Jeff said. He was being cautious. Clyde knew he was going to lose him soon if he couldn't keep up with America's pace. He seemed like a nice fella too.

They slid down a short bank, and a very long swinging bridge that seemed to go on forever came into view. Horses were bunched around the entrance to the heavy plank bridge. They drew closer, and America looked at the bridge suspiciously. He trotted through the group milling around trying to convince their animals onto the bridge. "Don't look over the side, boy, and it'll be ok. I'll do the same if it's ok with you," Clyde spoke quietly to America.

"Yep, just keep those big brown eyes front and center." Clyde was holding his breath again. America didn't hesitate as he leaped up and onto the wooden bridge.

Clyde's soothing voice had reassured America and bewildered the frustrated riders who watched them pass. They came clomping off the wood planking onto the rocky road.

"Lordy," Clyde said exhaling. He looked back over his shoulder. Jeff was coming on and the others were behind him.

"Guess they needed a teacher," Clyde laughed.

There were at least ten riders ahead taking up the entire roadway. One lady looked back and saw him coming.

"Fast rider approaching," she yelled to the others. They divided like the Red Sea. Clyde was feeling good, now that his adrenaline was pumping from the bridge crossing. America didn't break stride, and he didn't acknowledge the other horses. He was all business. Clyde smiled as they cleared the riders and he reached down and rubbed the stallion's shoulder. The stallion was breathing evenly, nostrils flaring. Clyde removed his feet from the stirrups, relaxing his legs and doing a stretch. "I'm stiff old boy," he said as America cantered. Clyde wondered if this horse could canter forever.

The remains of Deadwood lined the street of an old mining town. Rotting timbers and ruined foundations of buildings that had fallen down long ago dotted the landscape. That's where Jeff finally caught up with him again.

"Look there," Clyde pointed. "They had their mines right in the darn town. A wall of rock and shale was dotted with old tunnels, next to what looked to be Main Street.

"Sure enough," agreed Jeff. "You know this timber around here looks as though it was burned a long time ago.

"By golly, I think you're right. Maybe that's what finally got them all in the end," Clyde said. They left the ghost town to its memories and galloped out of town, heading for Michigan Bluff.

Michigan Bluff was high upon the Middle Fork and El Dorado Canyons, about two thousand feet above their respective rivers. It seemed to cling to the steep slopes it was lodged upon. Like the other ghost town, there were the remains of a short, but lively past.

"How in the world anyone ever got supplies into these places is amazing to me," Clyde said to Jeff.

"I reckon they just packed it all up here, one mule at a time." Jeff laughed.

"Look, there are a few places that have been fixed up and people are living in them." They trotted around five or six riders loosely strung down the roadway looking at the view.

"Sure is, looks like civilization," he laughed. "Look, Clyde, when we stop at the rest, I don't think I'll be able to keep up with you anymore. I'm afraid to push this girl too hard and you can go a heck of a lot faster. So don't worry about us. I just want to finish this ride with this old girl. That ok with you?"

"Sure." Clyde smiled. When they turned the corner they found the vet check. Clyde knew that Michigan Bluff was forty miles out. He knew what he had left to ride. He didn't know what it looked like, but they had been steadily dropping down onto lower elevations for the last several hours. It was getting noticeably warmer. The afternoon sun was fading, that worried him a mite. He would be an hour at this stop and the race would get tougher, if for no other reason, that horses and riders were weary. America was still strong and willing. They trotted in and stopped beside the farrier's truck. He wanted a complete check-up this time. The last part of the race would be crucial. He hadn't really had to ask for more from America, but that could change. So far, he had pretty much been sitting aboard as a passenger. Clyde was looking forward to one of his famous ten-minute naps; then he saw Joe.

Joe ran over and grabbed America's reins. The stallion began rubbing his head on Joe's shirt.

"That is not acceptable—but this is an exception," Joe told his horse, laughing.

Clyde swung off the horse and hugged Joe.

"Do you realize that you are in the top forty riders, dad?" Joe was frantic with excitement. Clyde looked around.

"That right?"

"Yep."

"Mercy," Clyde exhaled looking around again. "Guess we've been enjoyin' the scenery too much. Where'd they all go?"

"Oh here and there," Joe laughed. "Mostly behind you. Here you eat this." He handed Clyde a sandwich. "I'll take care of America, clean him off, feed and water him. You take a nap if you can."

"That's what I had in mind. Run him by the farrier, too, will you, son?"

"Right," Joe said. Clyde was already eating his sandwich and downing a Gatorade drink. Forty-five minutes later he was climbing aboard again.

"See you this evening, Lord willing and the creek don't rise." Clyde grinned and waved. He didn't know how true his words would prove to be. "By the way, we both want steak and a beer," he shouted over his shoulder. Joe gave him a thumbs-up. Then he shouted, "Be careful, looks like a storm brewin' over that way," and Joe pointed to the west. Clyde squinted up his eyes and looked at the big black cumulus clouds gathering on the western horizon.

"Don't need that, do we big guy?" he said to America. Clyde went down the dusty trail, and the orange and black vest flapping in the wind said number 254.

Joe told himself not to count the horses. He told himself that the number sequence that Clyde left in didn't matter. He counted them anyway. His father was the seventh rider leaving Michigan Bluff. Joe also told himself that a lot could change over the next five hours. He found himself saying a prayer. Why not, after all, it was his father and his horse. He heard the distant rumble of thunder and looked to the west. It was going to get bad out there. To top it off, the sun would be down soon.

Storm clouds opened on the riders about six o'clock, and Clyde couldn't see twenty feet in front of America. The sun was setting behind the clouds. Soon, it would be impossible to see. Here I am, a passenger again, thought Clyde. Well I always said this game had to do with trust. I guess I'll see if I was right. He had managed to pull his collar up and his hat down. Rain pelted both horse and rider. Lightening popped all around. The stones on the trail were wet and shiny. He could see them with every lightening strike. Puddles were forming and soon the trail would be a small stream, and he knew that they had to cross the American River up by Poverty Bar. "It sure wouldn't do to have that river at flood stage, now would it?" Clyde was asking God. Lightening struck and America flinched.

"Ok, Ok," Clyde said, "you heard me. Got the message." He hoped they wouldn't be electrocuted before they had at least a chance at finishing this thing. He didn't think he'd be up to this torture for too many more years. "We only need a chance," he mumbled. But, he knew the old Indian saying; "It is a good day to die." Fate had a way of intervening in man's quests for greatness.

They started into a steep descent that scared Clyde to death. America slid down the wet slope on his haunches and Clyde laid so far back over the horse's butt that he felt like he was doing the movie 'Man from Snowy River'. The switchbacks down the hill were sharp and treacherous, and at the bottom, a rocky rolling green stream. Clyde thought it was Volcano Creek. The stream was running full and the current was moving fast. Clyde was assessing it as they drew closer, but he never got the chance to make his decision. The stallion plunged into the swift current acting like he was out for a Sunday swim. The current almost knocked Clyde from the Calvary saddle. He grabbed for America's mane and hung on. Another horse at the halfway point in the stream was struggling against its rider. The guy had choked up on the reins and the horse couldn't get his neck out in front of him. The animal's eyes were showing a lot of white as the horse fought the rider and the swift current. It did not look promising for either one of them. America passed the struggling pair. The other rider looked at Clyde with horror on his face.

"Let up on him," Clyde screamed. As soon as the words came out of Clyde's mouth, the rider dropped his reins. At which time the poor horse regained his push against the water. They were behind him now and America struck solid ground. Maybe the pair would make it. Clyde focused ahead again as they bounded onto the gravely shore.

The forest was thick with huge pines and hardwoods hovering over them. They traveled swiftly through the pine straw. Only Clyde, through the sound of the rain, heard the horse's breathing and snorting. America cantered along as if he were on his way home. For all that Clyde knew, perhaps he knew this was the way home. Clyde could at least make out the trail as long as they had the protection of the forest. The rain filtering through the pines seemed to be to the stallion's liking. He was upon and past two riders before he even knew it.

"Hi." Clyde waved back to them.

"Hi," they hollered, watching the old man with the rain-slicked jacket, number 254 waving to them. Rain by the bucket pelted them as they entered Forest Hill Mill Site vet check. A guy with a big red umbrella holding his note pad was standing along the roadway. Clyde pulled America down to a walk. Clyde could see a community around the area. Lights flickered through the trees and the rain.

"We're concerned about the American River crossing," the vet said. "The guys at the dam are full up and they aren't able to shut off the water as usual. We've had too much rain over the last several weeks," he shouted to Clyde. "The run off might beat you to Provery Bar crossing. With luck it'll let up, but who knows." He smiled as water dripped from his big nose.

"Is the storm predicted to stop?" Clyde asked the vet as he checked America.

"Don't know, hard to tell up in these hills." After the vet check, he let America rest and eat. He contented himself by watching his horse lick his bucket clean.

"Guess nothing bothers your stomach, does it?" he asked America. Clyde had covered the stallion with a tarp provided by the vet so that America wouldn't chill as he rested. Well, he couldn't do anything about the weather. America seemed good to go. This horse was amazing, thirty-three miles out, and the best he could tell he was up with the fastest riders. He figured he was too darn old to die young, so they rode on at a gallop waving to the messenger. There must have been at lease a hundred folks lining the roadway all holding umbrellas and cheering. This is like a real town, he thought.

He wished the weather were clear; he would have enjoyed looking at the old town. They crossed a paved road that had stores on both sides of the roadway and began to descend down into the canyons again.

"This in from our man in the sky," the announcer on the intercom said. "There are ten riders leading the way out of Forest Hill Mill Site vet check. They are as follows in the order in which they left; number 233, Marjorie Welker riding Blaze A Fire, number 166, Bonnie Straite riding BB Thomas, number 67, Bob Beaucher riding My Clemontine, number 89, Betty Williams riding CLDodger, number 306, Hank Smith riding Fire N Ice, number 229, Candy Faust riding Sleeping Beauty, number 188, Troy Stuart riding Bint Baskalee, number 254, Clyde Richards riding America, number 122, Glenda Rodgers riding Steppen Out, If you all remember Glenda Rodgers was our first place winner last year. Also number 194, Tommy Williams riding MG Mega Man."

Joe ran to the pay phone. "D, you won't believe it."

"What Joe?"

"They are in the top ten coming out of Forest Hill. Dad is eighth. The announcer just relayed it from the helicopter pilot monitoring the race."

"No—you're kidding?" Denneyse said. "My gosh, can you believe this? I don't know about the rest of the way, but by golly we'll hear war stories about this for the rest of his life. That's wonderful, Joe. I'll bet you've no regret on letting Clyde ride now?"

"I didn't have regret anyway," Joe smiled. "I just can't wait to see him," Joe rushed on. I'll call you later and let you know what happens. Don't forget to call Susan and Cindi."

Clyde and America rounded a corner of the trail and came behind several riders. The lady in last place in the line was on a huge gray beast whose derriere did not outsize his rider. Clyde momentarily forgot his goal and his fatigue and was mesmerized by the site of her bottom rising and falling in unison with her horse's. How could a horse carry that much weight that far? He came back to reality when he realized that not only was it raining, but that he was sweating like a stuck pig under his waterproof jacket. Coming from 8,700 feet to 700 feet was a reality check. Thank goodness it was raining. To make matters worse, the wind was picking up. He reached for his water bottle and began gulping it. He imagined a cold beer that would greet him soon. He passed riders running in the middle of the trail. They did not look happy and their horses looked worse. They were a weary looking group.

An Egyptian legend Clyde had read once popped happily into his mind as America pushed gamely on. 'If the gray pursues, drop down into the desert floor. The gray will melt in the sun. If the black pursues, run on. The black will fade before the sun dips into the western sky, for he does not endure. But if the bay pursues, be afraid, and race on. Prepare to fight, for the bay is swift and tireless, he will find you.' Clyde reached over in mid-stride and rubbed America on the shoulder.

Clyde followed the road markers out of the gorge and entered Fords Bar. He pulled a peanut butter sandwich from his saddle pack and ate it as he rode him into the next check. America drank and then settled contentedly onto his portion of leafy hay. Clyde stretched out beside the horse on the ground with his hat over his face. Horses walked by him. People walked by him. In ten minutes exactly he was up and moving. Clyde Richards was a master at catnaps. He always joked with Joe about his catnaps saying that he was preparing for the BIG Sleep when he was caught napping. Joe didn't see the humor in it. It was a blessing this day, though.

He saw two riders leaving. He was quick to get mounted and America was willing enough to get on with the job at hand.

A man rode up beside him; "Can you believe that the gorge we came through was 110 degrees just before it started to rain?"

"Yes sir, I surely believe that." Clyde smiled.

By golly, first he froze and then he melted. There was not much chit chat between the riders now. It had quieted down noticeably. Conserve, he thought. He wasn't much of a talker anyway. Clyde was a little stiff getting back in the saddle. He'd have to do a few exercises as he rode. He was holding America at a trot coming across the valley floor. Provery Bar couldn't be far ahead. Since the rain, he was worried about the crossing. No sooner than he thought it, the rain started in again. Five miles further, it was taking a toll on his body. His hands were numb, and with the coming of darkness, his feet were beginning to feel as bad. The feel of the river surrounded him. The air was heavy and the ground that America was trotting through was nothing but muck and mush. Thick brush threatened to block the trail. The tall trees had become fewer and fewer until they had disappeared completely. Amazingly, he could still hear the deep-voiced bullfrogs through the rain. Suddenly, the river appeared. He pulled America back so quickly that the horse squatted on his haunches. The American River was at flood stage. The crossing markers were visible in the downpour. For a split second he had thought they got off the main trail, but the markers were there all right. America began spinning around on the bank, wanting to cross. Great rolls of waves were visible.

Clyde thought the waves were covering boulders hidden in the water. He could barely make out the other side.

"This is not good, old buddy," he said to America trying to steady the horse long enough to figure something out. America kept turning in the mud and Clyde was deep in thought when a girl on a horse pushed past him and plunged into the swollen river.

"Hey," Clyde yelled. He watched with rising fear as the girl's horse fought the current. She was afloat and traveling down stream fast. He knew she was in trouble.

"Ah crap," he yelled, and put his heels to America's sides and plunged into the water after her.

She went down into the muddy water and was swallowed. He saw her horse's head, wild eyed and wet. He saw her head; her hair long and dark as it swirled around her. He didn't know if he could reach her in time. He was exhausted. He hoped he had enough in him to get to her. Clyde had his right hand on his reins and his left entangled in America's mane. As they came alongside the girl, he dropped his reins and held out his right hand to her. She went under, then came up gasping and coughing. My god, but she looked like his Peggy. Why—how could his Peggy be here? The lightening flashed.

"My hand," he screamed at her. "Take my hand." She looked into his eyes, her face filled with terror.

"Grab it now," he screamed, moving his big calloused hand out as far as he could without falling from the saddle. She reached. They clasped hands.

"Come on Peg," he moaned, "pull, pull." America swam; water flew from his nostrils as he struggled for the bank. The water tore at the girl trying to suck her under.

Peg's face lit up in the light. It was Peg's face smooth and wet and afraid. How could this be?

"Come on, we got it," he screamed at her. Clyde pulled for all he was worth. Suddenly the river let her go and she was behind him, her arms wrapped tight around his waist. America had his footing and bounded ashore in a leap. Clyde had all he could do to pull the horse back.

"Whoa bud, whoa," he shouted to the horse. America stopped. The girl slid down.

"Hey," Clyde pointed, "there's your horse. Her horse had climbed out of the river and stood, head down, tail tucked by a clump of shrub not twenty-five feet away.

"Thanks mister," the girl stuttered. She was shivering.

"What's your name," she yelled up to him.

"Clyde," he said. "It's Clyde Richards."

"I thought it was over for me, Clyde, till you came along. You meet friends in strange places these days. Thanks," she smiled. "My name is Glenda." Her smile was wet and slick but it lit her dainty face. It wasn't Peggy. He knew he'd gone 'round the bend. Seconds ticked by. The girl spun on her heels, and yelled, "Let's go." She ran to her horse. She looked like a small wet boy with long dark hair from the rear.

"We're almost home," she said, as she took off on the weary half-drowned animal that had waited for her. The rain was letting up. He could see some distance ahead now. He didn't think he liked doing this dern stuff in the dark much. It made a body see things that weren't there. Gave him the creeps too.

As they crossed a highway, he began to feel woozy. His adrenaline rush was over. He knew it must be Highway 49 at the Rock Quarry. There were plenty of people around making sure horses and cars didn't meet.

He crossed a concrete bridge about one hundred feet long. America's shoes hitting the concrete had a comforting rhythm, and he was thankful for the dark. He didn't want to see what he was crossing, he wanted to rest. He was tired and he realized that he had never felt this tired in his entire life. He wished that he had done this ride thirty years earlier. Nothing would have been able to stop him thirty years ago. Even ten years ago—I was near bullet proof till I was fifty. Well I'm not fifty any more. I'm sixty-two and if I don't get my butt moving, I'm not going to get another chance. Besides, I wouldn't have had America ten years ago. He smiled as they hit the dirt road beyond the bridge and America went into a canter. A rider came rushing by and knocked into them almost pushing them from the roadway.

"Thanks," Clyde yelled after the guy. The horse's rider was clinging to the animal's neck trying to regain his stirrups. Clyde turned in the saddle. Two more riders were coming on. He squeezed America's sides. They were close to the second rider, but he knew that lingering at the river had lost him the chance to regain his advantage. What an old fool, he was thinking he had seen his Peggy. Ah, well, he thought, and smiled.

At 10:38 Glenda Rodgers crossed the finish line. She rode to first place at a record time of seventeen hours and thirty-eight minutes. Second place went to Hank Smith. Hank was a ten-time contender at the Tevis. Clyde Richards was third by ten lengths.

EPILOGUE

The next afternoon at the awards ceremony:
"Come on up here Glenda. You've done it again." Everyone was gathered around. A whole pig was roasting on a covered barbecue. There were tables and tables of food.

"Two times in a row and at the record time of seventeen hours and thirty-eight minutes. What a ride," the announcer yelled into the mike. "Let's hear it for a great little lady." Clapping and cheering sounded throughout the park. They were gathered under a big army tent. The sun was out full. The rain had pushed over the Sierra Nevada's and it had been a crystal clear day, although Clyde had slept through half of it. They were still a haggard looking bunch. The tent reminded Clyde of a good old Southern Baptist revival tent and he felt he needed some reviven' too.

"If this guy doesn't get on with it, I believe I'll just lay down right here." Clyde said. Joe who was giddy with excitement was standing at his elbow.

"Glenda," the announcer went on, "That makes two of these silver cups. Are you going to build a special shelf to hold them all?"

Glenda stood on tiptoes and got the microphone away from the announcer. She looked strong for a small person, Clyde thought.

"I would like to say something before we get further into our ceremony." The folks gathered around and got quiet. Clyde could see Genda's hands were shaking as she held onto the microphone. "I'd like to say thanks to all of you nice folks. It has been great being a part of a bunch like this. I mean it," she said. More cheers erupted. "Horse people are a real special group of people. They look out for one another, just like they look out for their horses. I want you all to recognize a special horse person, Clyde Richards." She looked at Clyde. Clyde's eyes got big. "Clyde, please come up here." He walked up and stood beside Glenda. "Clyde is our third place rider." Glenda reached over and pulled Clyde over a little closer. "I met Clyde for the very first time last night in the middle of the American River." Laughter moved around the group. "Believe me it wasn't funny. I've got to say I don't recommend meeting like we did last night. Anyway, I want to give this gentleman my silver cup. Now I know what the rules say and I know what the regulations are. This gentleman would have been first place had he not stopped in the middle of the American River and saved my life. I am a very, very lucky lady to be alive this evening. If this man and his stallion had not of had the courage to pluck me from the river—well I sure wouldn't be standing here right now." Glenda smiled up at Clyde. "The cup is yours, Clyde, I say so." Glenda reached up and kissed Clyde's cheek. They both had tears in their eyes as the roar of the crowd broke out. Glenda stretched up on her tiptoes and whispered in his ear. "I expect a reasonable stud fee for my mare, Clyde Richards." When she pulled back, she winked at him.

"Clyde Richards, you had yourself an adventure," Rose Gillard beamed at him. She gave him a bear hug. He'd just loaded America into the trailer. They were packing up after a day's rest. It was time to get on the road.

"Rose, I see you got yourself one of those silver buckles. By golly, I sure hope you didn't commit a crime getting it," Clyde laughed.

"Can you believe it," she squealed. "We got in here in twenty hours and fifty-six minutes. Not bad for an old woman. I got my buckle fair and square."

"Nope, that is not bad at all," Clyde laughed.

"You have the Cup?" she smiled.

"Glenda won't take it back," he shrugged.

"I guess not. I wouldn't either. You're some kind of heros—you and that stallion of yours. I think we'll be seeing a lot more of the likes of him. Maybe you can squeeze out some of those warm bloods back there in Carolina?"

"You know you California folks aren't so bad," Clyde grinned.

"Why, Clyde Richards, you South Carolinians aren't so bad either." She smiled.

Clyde stuck a fresh toothpick in his mouth and saluted to her. Clyde climbed into the truck beside Joe. Joe was shaking his head.

"You got to watch messing with older women, you know."

"Yeah," Clyde agreed. About fifteen minutes later as they were pulling onto Highway 80 heading east, "That Calvary saddle is the real deal son. My granddaddy would have been proud."

Joe accelerated to seventy and pushed on the cruise control.

"I talked to Susan. She is having this huge party for us. The whole dern town is coming Saturday night to her house."

"That's Susan. She's a sweet heart, but she does like to throw a party. She's always flitten here and flitten there. She's a gull darn butterfly. Here, I just want to sit on the porch and rock." Clyde looked disappointed. He was thinking he wanted to rock and remember his ride one hoof beat at a time. He wanted to get all the memories filed away proper before his old brain started forgetten them all. He didn't want to chance his memories floaten off somewhere, god knows where.

"Oh, and I talked to Doc. Georgee's hoof is as good as new, and she's in foal."

"Ha," Clyde laughed. "Good. That is good. What a time I've had. Thank you son," he said as they watched the Sierra Nevadas fade from view.

Home at last. He would simply take his shower and fall into bed. The drive home had exhausted him. That was the only plan that he had when he entered the cabin that night at 11 p.m.

He saw the message light blinking on the telephone. He had messages. Sitting in his boxer shorts on the edge of his bed, he pushed the message button.

"Hi, Joe, this is Cindi. Just wanted to congratulate you all on the wonderful performance in California. Call me when you have time. Talk to you soon. Bye." Joe was smiling. Joe looked at the read out on the message system. Good grief, there were eight more messages.

"Hey, honey. You guys were so wonderful. Call me even if it's two in the morning. Love you, bye," Denneyse said. Joe was shaking his head laughing.

"Hi Joe, this is Dave at the Feed 'n Seed. Way to go. Wanted to congratulate you is all. The whole blamed town has gone plum nuts over you and your horse. I want to use you both in a feed advertisement for our store. Call me when you can. Bye."

"Hello this is Sandra Williams from Greeley, Colorado. I would like to talk to you about breeding our mare next March. Please give me a call at 903-526-4498. Thank you."

And so it went. There were four local congratulation calls; the rest were questions for stud services. Joe was sitting, staring at the telephone, when suddenly it rang.

"Hello," Joe said. "Yes he's my horse." Joe looked at his watch. It was 12.30 EST. "Yes sir, that was my father riding. Yes sir," Joe laughed. "It was some kind of ride alright. Yes, I'll be here this weekend. Saturday? Sure. Well, as soon as you get in, give me a call and I'll come on over to the airport and pick you up. Ok, good, I'll look forward to it. Yes, thank you." Joe hung up the telephone, then immediately picked it up again and dialed D's number.

"I'm home."

"Good," she yawned. "I was waiting for your call. Gosh, Joe, what a great win. Clyde was wonderful. He's a hero clear across the country and everyone here is planning this huge party. America's five years old and he's already famous. I just can't believe it."

"I can't believe it either. Dad was way beyond wonderful. Wait until you guys see the pictures. I just got a call from a Mr. Roy Harris in Austin, Texas. He's flying up Saturday morning just to see America. He raises Egyptian Arabians in Austin and has twelve mares to breed next February. He wants to see this horse called America for himself. He says a good friend of his, the father of Glenda Rodgers, no less, was privy to the news that there was a legend in the making in the horse world. The horse seemed to appear out of nowhere." Joe laughed at that. "But he thought it was time South Carolina got somewhere in the Arabian horse world. Glenda told her father Sam that she predicted this horse America would win everything there was to win in the endurance world. Roy Harris said that if Glenda said this was going to happen, it must be true. He wants to see this horse first hand. Says that's the way they did business in Texas. Get this D," he said, "he wants in on some of this new Arab blood." Joe was laughing. "America's pedigree goes to desert bred quicker than any pedigree I've ever seen. Seems having the oldest blood in the pedigree has suddenly become new. Doc will be excited about all of this. We are sure going to need her help now. The best way for a stallion to prove his worth is through his prodigy. Looks like he's going to have plenty of opportunity."

"Joe, will you be able to quit your job up there and come to the ranch now? Maybe we could make a go of it with all the stud fees." Denneyse sounded excited.

"Let's see how it goes. It's looking more and more like a job opportunity in Camden, isn't it?"

The mares were lining up at America's stall door. Man, Joe sighed. What a grievous problem for a stallion.

Their love for one another and their horses were a fact. They were married in a quiet ceremony at the ranch in Camden, S.C. in the winter of 1996.

The cabin in Greenville was sold for a hefty profit when he discovered from the Forestry Service that his property was the sole entrance to Hidden Falls. The U.S. Government immediately decided that they needed to purchase his property to protect the area for future generations. They now use the cabin that Joe built for the ranger's quarters. The barn that America was born in is now the home of the ranger's horse Pete.

Jessica Langley Richards, (the Langley from Joe's mother's family) was born eleven months after the wedding.

"Darn good thing, too," Clyde teased. "I still have my granddaddy's double barrel shotgun."

Jessie was the apple of Grandpa Richards's eye. Everyone in Camden knew Jessie. She always rode shotgun in her Grandpa's old blue into town with him.

They were sitting on the porch of the ranch house in the swing. Denneyse was patting Joe's knee. It was just getting on to dusk. And the Cicadas were beginning their evening song.

She giggled, "Remember what you said to Mr. Humpries, Joe?"

"I still can't believe that I actually said something like that to a CEO," he smiled.

"Yep, you strolled into Mr. Humpries office, the Office of Human Resource Management and said, and I quote,

'Mr. Humpries, I've been an engineer coming up on two years now. Mr. Humpries, my boss, is a company man; my boss's boss is a company man. With all due respect sir, I am not a company man. I just want to go to Camden and ride my horse, sir.'"

"That's right." Joe shook his head. "It's true, too. I've never regretted it for a minute."

The nightlights were beginning to flicker on. They were watching Jessica play with her Grandpa.

"This is heaven," he said to her quietly. The creaky old swing they sat in was hanging from the original eyebolts that Joe's grandfather had screwed into the roof of the porch. Some things should not change, unless it couldn't be helped.

"This is truly heaven," he sighed. "I really don't care if I ever go down the driveway again, unless it's with you and Jessie and America.

"Well, looks like you won't have to; they're all coming down our driveway to see America. You can just stay here and wait for them," she smiled.

Jessie threw the ball to her Grandpa. Grandpa tossed it back. The air was still and hot. It was a typical muggy Carolina evening. Rain threatened, as it tended to do every evening this time of year. Clyde picked up the ball that Jessie had thrown to him.

"Hey kiddo, Grandpa's real hot. It's too hot to play ball, Jessie. Come sit a while on the porch with your Grandpa. Let's rest awhile darlin'." Clyde was walking to the porch when Denneyse called to Jessie.

"Leave your Grandpa alone now sweetheart."

She walked over and handed Clyde a cool glass of fresh lemonade, then went into the house with Joe. Clyde settled into the oversized wicker chair and got comfortable. The porch fan was whirling overhead and his thin hair blew in the breeze. Jessie came up the steps, then ran to the chair Clyde was in and climbed into his lap.

"Gimme a drink please?" she asked. Jessie slurped the glass almost dry.

"Here, you hold it," she shoved the empty glass back into his big hand and snuggled closer to him. Looking out from the porch they could still see into the pasture behind the house where America and his girls were contently clipping grass. The fading light reflected hints of gold and red in the horses' coats as they moved past the glow from the nightlight in the yard.

"Granny, can we go sit on the fence and watch America?" Jessica begged. She was three, but already wanted to be near the horses. Clyde smiled down at her and ruffled the brown curly hair. The child smelled like sunshine and sweat. Her little compact body was soft and cuddly.

"Let's just sit awhile Jessie, I'll tell you a story. It's too hot to go out there just now," Clyde answered.

"Ok. Can it be a very good story Granny?"

"Yes, Clyde smiled. "A very good story." Jessie swung her legs up and lay her head down in her grandfather's lap, then looked up at him with big blue eyes.

"Don't make me sleep," she warned.

"Not on your life, honey. This is an important story and I want you to hear all of it."

In a few minutes she was almost asleep. Clyde was looking out in the pasture at the fading light when he stopped and stared at the black mare standing by the fence. He saw a beautiful lady standing beside the mare. The lady was waving to him. He knew she was waving to him. There was no one on the porch but he and Jessie. The lady had a straw bonnet in her hand. Clyde raised himself up in the chair. My lord, it was Peg. The more he tried to focus on the woman the more his eyes grew watery. He dabbed at his eyes, trying to clear his vision so that he could see the woman more clearly when she began walking away, motioning him to come on. There were glints of gold gleaming in the woman's dark hair.

"Peggy?" he said. Jessie sat up.

"Hey Grandpa, who is that lady?"

"Jessica, sweetie, you lay back down here until your mother comes out of the house for you. Promise me?"

"Where are you going Gramp?" she frowned.

Clyde stood up carefully arranging Jessie on the chair cushions. He thought that he understood now. At the Tevis cup, in the river when he had seen her and she had helped him. She was close then and looking out for him. Helping him finish up his time with dignity. What a lady his Peg was. He smiled at Jessie. She would be another special lady like his Peg had been.

"You close your eyes and rest Jessie, promise?"

"Oh, Ok, I promise," she said slowly. Her voice faded and the warmth of the evening worked its magic as sleep pressed down on her small body. Her mother's cool hand touching her cheek woke her.

"Where is Grandpa Jessie?" Denneyse smiled at her.

"Out there," Jessie pointed sleepily, "with the pretty lady," she said rubbing her eyes with her hand.

"What pretty lady Jessie?"

"Don't know, Grandpa said the name Peggy." Jessie looked up at her mother. "Gramp got tired of telling me a story and he made me lay down for forty winks until you came." Jessie made a face, blinking her eyes and laughing. "Then the pretty lady came and called him and he went out there. I saw Gramp dance with the lady," she giggled. "I must have winked too hard. I couldn't see them anymore. Mama is that the pretty lady that Gramp says I am like?"

"Yes Jessie, I believe it was." Denneyse said as she looked at Joe.

***

Printed in the United States
1669